DEADLY SPELLS AND A SOUTHERN BELLE

BELLES AND SPELLS MATCHMAKER MYSTERY
BOOK ONE

AMY BOYLES

LADYBUGBOOKS LLC

DEADLY SPELLS
AND A
SOUTHERN BELLE

AMY BOYLES

ONE

$\mathcal{I}$ always considered my life as being presented in neat little packages. There's a box for getting up, one for going to work, returning home and such. My life is normal, mundane, all of the above.

If I had been told that, on a certain day, everything in my world would turn topsy-turvy, I would have said the likelihood of that happening was one million, three hundred thousand, twenty-six to one.

That's how confident I was—at least I had been when I woke up.

And if someone had also said that I would answer the phone and my mother would be on the line, I would reply that the odds of that were much smaller, more like one hundred to one, since she called at least once a week—mostly to tell me how I was failing as a daughter.

Sigh. Don't get me wrong, my mother and I love each other, but I spent the first half of my life trying to please her.

Nothing ever worked.

Growing up, all I ever heard was that Glinda Calhoun—yes, that Glinda, as in my mother was named after the good witch in *The Wizard of Oz*—was the most talented witch to have lived in the past fifty years.

I heard countless stories about how she had vanquished the fire trolls with a wall of water, and how, when a Pegasus herd had needed to migrate to South America, my mother had created a fog that shielded them from being seen.

I mean, what would normal people do if they knew mythological creatures existed?

Oh yes, I'd been regaled with stories of Mama all my life.

Which was why I grew up desperately trying to please her. One Christmas I had an entire spell planned. I would make it snow on Christmas Eve.

So what if we lived in the Deep South and it never, or at least rarely, snowed, and when it did, it was only a dusting that melted within an hour? I could still do it.

That night I called my mother over to the window, raised my hands and worked the spell for snow.

A single snowflake fell on the window and melted.

That was it.

My mother patted my shoulder and sighed. "It's no use, Charming. You simply weren't born with the magic that I was. I suppose I sucked that lemon dry, leaving you with only a pittance of power. But rest assured, darling." She bent down, meeting me at eye level and gently tapping my forehead. "Your brain is better suited to math and science. There's nothing wrong with that—unless you're a witch as gifted as me, of course."

Then she shooed me off to work on my homework. But it wasn't all bad because I eventually figured out that I could mix magic and math, which eventually led to a lucrative career as a matchmaker.

So that's how it was my whole life. My magic was small, a single candle flame quaking in the wind of her tsunami of power.

But that was years ago and I've had twenty-eight years to grow up. I was currently driving down I-65, headed to the wedding of two soul mates I had successfully introduced.

My phone beeped, telling me I had a message. I pressed the button and listened.

"Charming, it's Jimmy."

I frowned. Jimmy Valdez was my best employee. He made any challenge seem like a walk in a meadow. If I had to tell two people who hated one another that they were each other's soul mates, Jimmy always took the reins, easing folks into the situation like silk.

"There's something strange going on at Witch's Forge. It's weird. I think you might have to—"

Then the message ended. Frowning, I glanced at the date. The message was from a couple of days ago, but it hadn't pinged me until today.

Stupid phone.

A thought niggled the back of my mind. It wasn't like Jimmy to be worried about a project. I pressed the button to dial his number. The phone rang, but there was no answer.

I'd just set my phone down when it rang again. Thinking it was Jimmy calling me back, I hit the Talk button on my steering wheel.

I instantly regretted it.

Remember, I told you the odds were small that Mama would call.

"Hello?"

"Charming, darling, it's Mama."

My mother's delicate Southern-accented voice filtered into the cabin.

The fresh air I had been inhaling suddenly seemed restrictive, like I was choking on it. Happened every time I spoke to her.

I rolled up the window.

"How are you, Mama?"

"Oh, I'm simply marvelous. I am at a wonderful convention in Nepal teaching water witches new spells that will help them find drinking water."

"How great for them," I murmured.

"Charming, you don't know how much these people need me."

"Leave it to a white woman to think she can save the world."

"Don't be like that," she said quickly. "If you practiced your magic on something other than matchmaking, you might have more skill."

"You sure about that?"

She considered it for a moment. "No, I suppose not."

"And there you have it," I grumbled.

"I suppose since I was gifted with so much magic, it was destined that you would only have a token of my gift."

I clenched my teeth. "No need to brag."

"Can you hear me?"

"Loud and clear."

"I'm using one of those satellite phones. The darned thing is so strange and static filled. Really, darling, I wish you would just let me use magic when I need to contact you."

This old argument. I clenched my teeth. "Because I live in the human world and an apparition of a talking and floating head might scare people."

She snorted. "You might live in the human world but you help witches and wizards find their soul mates. By the way, how is your little business going?"

I rolled my eyes. "*My little business* just got a huge contract. We're matching the entire town of Witch's Forge."

"Witch's Forge?" It sounded like she gasped. "That dreadful place. Stay away from it."

I quirked a brow. "Why? Is there too much magic there for me?"

"Witch's Forge is a dead town," she explained. "In its heyday it was wonderful, but since certain…things happened, the town has been suffering a slow death. The spells the witches who live there cast backfire. Can you imagine?" She quickly answered her own question. "Probably not. That's not something you'd understand, Charming. Anyway, it's probably best you're not in that heathen town. The place is like death. It would more than likely suck the rest of your magic out of you."

"Thank you." I rolled my eyes. "Anyway, I sent Jimmy."

"Oh, Jimmy," she cooed. "How is that wonderful young man? He's just such a bright star. I remember last time I came to your office. That dear boy gave me flowers and chocolate."

Months ago, when Jimmy had discovered that my mother was coming to the office for lunch, he nearly had a panic attack.

"Your mom is one of the greatest witches to have ever lived. What was it like growing up under her roof?"

It was Hades, actually.

Jimmy hadn't waited for my answer. "In college we studied her water wall spell," he gushed. "It was a thing of beauty. The way that she used it to surround a city in order to keep out the fire trolls was amazing. Oh my gosh. And I hear she's off to help the people of Chile with their magic. What a saint."

Yep. My mother had a reputation I would never be able to live up to.

After that, Jimmy ran out to purchase flowers and chocolates.

My mother's crisp voice jarred me back to the present. "Charming? Are you there?"

"Jimmy is a darling," I said. "But he just left me a message—"

"You should date him."

My stomach seized. Jimmy was my friend but not boyfriend material.

I cleared my throat. "Listen, Mama, the reception is bad. That satellite phone is going in and out."

"Ugh, stupid human gadgets. Bye now. I'll talk to you soon, darling."

I jabbed the End Call button.

My mother was right, Witch's Forge was dying. That's why the mayor had contracted my company—Southern Belles and Spells Matchmakers. She hoped that making folks fall in love would revive the place.

Good luck to her.

After all, Witch's Forge was tucked away in the Great Smoky Mountains of Tennessee. Visiting a Podunk town riddled with country bumpkin witches was not my idea of a good time. Hence, why I'd sent Jimmy for the job.

My phone rang again. Still hoping it was Jimmy, I answered. "Southern Belles and Spells Matchmakers, this is Charming."

The woman's voice on the other end was frantic. "Charming! Oh goodness, I'm so glad I've reached you."

5

If there was one thing I hated, it was drama on a Saturday.

I cringed. Fires on the weekend were no good. But I was the leader of my company, and it was my job to put them out. So I threw my shoulders back and said, "And who is this?"

"This is Winnifred Dixon," she said.

"Who?"

"The mayor of Witch's Forge."

"Oh, right. What can I do for you, Mayor?"

"Can you hear me?"

I rolled my eyes. "Yes, I can hear you."

"There's a lot of static. Always is when I make calls outside of town."

"What is it? Mayor?"

"Oh, you're still there."

What was it with witches and phones? Didn't they know how to use them?

"Yes, ma'am. What can I do for you?"

"You sent your man Jimmy here to do our matchmaking, but no one can find him."

"What do you mean, he's missing?"

A bad feeling crept over my skin, making me shiver. First, the call from Jimmy he'd placed two days ago. He hadn't called me back, and my call hadn't gone through.

Her pitch reached an octave that I would describe as way past panic. "A couple of nights ago Jimmy said he was going to do some research. He hasn't returned. I'm afraid something has happened to him. I'm afraid he's dead. Charming, we need you to come to Witch's Forge."

So many thoughts whirled in my head. The first was that I didn't want to go to a Podunk town. The second was my mother's suggestion that I was a magical failure—that my *little business* was pointless.

The third and fiercest thought was that Jimmy was my friend. I had to find him, not just for me but for him.

The mayor's panic shifted to me, burying itself in my chest like a tick. It unfurled, and my cheeks burned.

If the world discovered that my company had sent an employee to match people with their soul mates and that said employee had gone missing, first off, no one would want to work for me. But then people also couldn't trust me. Who would trust Charming Calhoun to find their soul mate when I couldn't even keep my employees safe?

With Jimmy gone, someone had to take up the slack at Witch's Forge. My company couldn't afford to lose this contract. The work had to be done, because if it wasn't, that would be the end of Southern Belles and Spells Matchmakers.

I would be finished.

I glanced at my watch. If I skipped the wedding, I would arrive just after nightfall. I hated to miss it, but this was an emergency.

"Mayor, have a place ready for me to sleep. I'll be there tonight."

TWO

a wall of water poured like fury in front of me. My headlights bored into it but didn't penetrate. To the right and left, the only thing I could see was water.

I gripped the steering wheel and leaned forward, looking up.

"Yep, more water. Great."

Sheets of it fell so thick and fast it looked solid.

"As the magic in Witch's Forge became broken," Jimmy had explained to me before he left a little over a week ago, "a huge waterfall slowly sprouted up, eventually closing the town off from humans." He'd pulled the information from the World Wide Witch Web. "Before then, Witch's Forge was a thriving tourist town. Humans and nonhumans mingled."

I remember looking up from my computer screen. "How easy is it to get through?"

"Pretty easy, apparently." Jimmy traced a finger over the screen of his handheld tablet. "It's only a barrier to humans."

I eyed him skeptically. "A waterfall that will keep out humans? Must be something to see."

Now I realized the falls were no joke. Water misted up from the ground, surrounding my little Mini Cooper. The sound roared in my ears, and the vibration pounded deep in my chest.

"Well, Charming," I murmured to myself, "if you're ever going to gain an ounce of respect from your mother and save your company, you'd better just do it."

I gritted my teeth, brushed a strand of hair away from my face and pressed the accelerator.

The car inched forward. I had the feeling when I left Witch's Forge, I'd be calling my insurance company and claiming hail pummeled my car.

If you were a better witch, you could fix it yourself. That's what my mother would have said.

Yep, Mama tended to live in my head. I always heard her voice at the wrong time.

Like when I was kissing a boy. Not a man, a boy. I hadn't kissed a man in so long I only remembered them as boys.

It was awful. He'd be going in for the lips, and Mama's voice would pop in, *Charming, are you sure you're good enough for him?*

It never failed—I would jerk away and kill the moment.

Yes, you could say I had mommy issues.

But not anymore. Dagnabbit, this was my chance to leave her behind, to make a name for myself and prove that I might not have much magical talent, but my work was important.

I cocked my head, calculating the chance that I might be crushed from the water—three hundred, twelve thousand, six hundred and fifty to one.

Not bad.

I inched forward until the rain fired against my hood. It sounded like a thousand gunshots exploding. It hammered so hard my car's rear end lifted.

Time to get this over with.

I floored the accelerator and zoomed into the waterfall. The cabin immediately darkened as the falls engulfed me. The thundering sound of water filled my ears.

I gulped down a deep breath, ignoring the humidity that had taken over the cabin. Sweat dripped down my face and my hands trembled. Now was not the time to be afraid of being locked inside my car.

My eyes widened as I saw what I thought was a face greeting me. I shook my head and realized it was nothing more than some sort of weird-looking Wanted poster caught in the falls.

"That's weird," I mumbled.

I finally burst through, exhaling a deep breath that I hadn't realized I'd been holding. My knuckles were white. I loosened my grip on the wheel and sank back onto the leather seat.

For the first time in my life, I took a look at Witch's Forge.

It was nighttime, but the town's Main Street was lit up. A four-lane highway stretched for miles. A quick inventory of closed shops revealed that when Witch's Forge had been jamming, it had really been jamming.

At least half a dozen pancake houses lined both sides of the road while a huge witch figurine stood on top of a building proclaiming to be the Witch's Cauldron Wax Museum.

Across the highway sat the nightly live show of the Witchfields and McCoys, this area's version of the feuding Hatfields and McCoys. The building was so large it took up one whole corner of the block.

There was also a sign for a local theme park, Witchywood, and another store that looked like a castle, complete with a dragon coiled atop, called Witch Quest. A billboard advertised that at Witch Quest you could go on your very own fairy-tale quest by becoming magical and saving a princess or a prince.

I took a deep inhale. Wow, at one point this town had been covered up with tourists.

My Cooper idled at the crossroads of four interlocking streets—Earth Avenue, Water Street, Wind Avenue and Fire Street.

The four elements of witches. I am a watered-down water witch. My magic tends to be more systematic, while plenty of other witches work on feelings.

If feelings were how folks experienced magic, maybe that's why I wasn't very good at it. With a mother who did nothing but banter on about feelings, I got pretty tired of exploring them.

I prefer things to be more reliable, which is why my power works mathematically—why I developed a precise magical questionnaire that brings together two soul mates. A questionnaire that I might add works perfectly one hundred percent of the time.

Always.

I stared at the street corner. Though the lamps burned, most of the buildings in town were dark, but even in the dim light I could see the cracks, the way they were crumbling.

Kudzu grew on the storefronts, creeping down onto the sidewalks. Seeing all that icky greenery made my shoulders itch. Ew. Someone should really do something about the state of downtown.

A light glowed in a storefront. The mayor had promised to meet me. I assumed that's where she was.

I parked the car and headed inside. It was summer. The humidity was thick. Sweat immediately sprinkled my brow. I pulled my hair from the nape of my neck and inhaled the sweet scent of honey-suckles.

At least there was one good thing about this town.

I opened the door. A bell fixed above the frame tinkled, and a small, plump woman in her midfifties waddled up. She wore her hair short and curly. Gray streaked the tendrils at her temples, and her eyeglasses rested on a chain at her ample bosom.

She cocked a graying eyebrow at me. "Charming?"

"Yes, ma'am, that's me."

She sighed and approached, arms outstretched, as if I held the answer to all her problems. "Charming, you don't know how good it is to see you." She clasped my hand in both of hers. "I'm Winnifred Dixon, mayor of Witch's Forge."

"Great to meet you, Mayor." I took a moment to stare into her emerald eyes. They were filled with honesty and relief, though a mountain of worry was sprinkled in there, too.

I smiled warmly. "Tell me everything."

"I'll tell you more in the morning, when we officially meet. For now, let's get you settled into your house."

I cocked an interested brow. "House?"

I lived in a condo. It was great but small. Not that I needed a lot of space—I did not.

The mayor led me out the front door. "Yes, it's where Jimmy was staying."

I glanced at the rundown buildings. "This town used to really be something, huh?"

The mayor snorted. "Absolutely, and the only reason why Witch's Forge even flourished to begin with was because of the Bigfoot rumors."

"Bigfoot?" I nearly tripped over my own feet. "You're kidding."

She shook her head briskly. "Not at all. Supposedly the first settlers wiped out the population—that's if you believe the witch history books. Anyway, the creatures haven't been seen in these parts for years. But still, the legend persists."

The mayor grinned. "And tourists love legends and the possibility of sightings."

I didn't particularly like the idea of a Bigfoot sighting, but I stayed quiet.

The mayor exhaled a breath. "Anyway, maybe the house will show you something that will help us find Jimmy."

I frowned, confused. "Maybe the house will show me something? Mayor, what are you talking about?"

I followed her down the deserted street, being sure to avoid the creeping kudzu that looked to want to strangle anything in its path.

"You'll see."

I stopped to think about that, but the mayor continued on, keeping a brisk pace.

I rushed to catch up with her.

"You see how our town is—oh, mind the kudzu. It'll bite you if you're not careful."

Bite me? I lifted my leg. "Why doesn't someone do something about it? Y'all are witches and wizards, after all."

"We can't," she explained. "It's part of the problem here. Charming, I explained that the town is broken. The magic in it is drying up. If I want to resurrect the way Witch's Forge used to be in its heyday, then we have to bring the magic back."

The more I stared at the crumbling buildings, the more I realized it would take a miracle from the Almighty to make that happen.

Either way, I would still get paid.

The mayor stopped abruptly. "Ah, here we are." Her arm swept out in front of her. "Your new home away from home."

My gaze followed. Looming over me stood an empire-style building with a clock tower secured in the center. It sat just off the main four-lane, taking up its own patch of land.

I tipped my head from side to side, trying to puzzle this thing out. "Is that the courthouse?"

Mayor Dixon climbed the steps. Her heels clacked against the concrete. "It used to be. At one time the library was housed here. It was converted to a home years ago, but people say there are still a slew of books inside—if the house lets you find them."

I laughed nervously. "You make it sound like the house is alive."

She pulled an elaborate silver key from her pocket, shoved it in the lock and twisted it to the right. "Oh, it is. Jimmy thought it most intriguing. It's about the only magic that still works correctly in this town. For instance, if I try to light a match with my power, it won't work. See?"

The mayor yanked a stick from a nearby bush and chanted silently. Instead of the stick flaming, it turned to ice.

"Townsfolk can't work magic the way we used to."

She tossed the branch aside and opened the door, revealing darkness that reminded me of a cavernous mouth. The scent of must trickled up my nose. I sucked in my breath.

I wasn't one to be frightened of things like ghosts or darkness, but there was something heavy in the air of the place.

A cool wind whisked across my shoulders. I rubbed them, fighting the dread that threatened to take over.

Winnifred stepped inside, heels clacking. Gaslights flared to life, revealing a hall rich with lush teal brocade wallpaper, a darkly finished oak bannister and staircase and, well, that was it.

I took a step back outside and glanced left and right. There were windows and wings. Granted they were covered in kudzu like just about everything else in this town, but they existed.

When I stepped back inside, all I saw were the staircase and walls.

Winnifred understood my confusion. "The building has a mind of its own. It will reveal rooms to you as it sees fit."

I grimaced. "What if it doesn't like me?"

She laughed. It was a rich belly laugh, a deep chuckle that made me like her. "It will like you. Of course it will. Now, let me show you Jimmy's room." She lowered her voice. "That is, if the house hasn't changed it."

I wanted to slap my forehead. What had I gotten myself into?

I trudged up the stairs behind Winnifred, questioning why I ever took this job to begin with. As I walked, the gaslights flickered. They seemed to mock me as they danced side to side as if saying the house had all the answers but I would never know any of them.

"Here we are." Winnifred turned the knob and pushed but nothing happened. She gave me a sidelong glance. "The house may be preparing for a female visitor. Did the same thing when I brought Jimmy. It wouldn't let us in for a moment."

The walls shuddered. They tightened and condensed. My skin did the same. I scraped my nails along the wall, trying to find something to hold on to.

Winnifred took one look at me and laughed. "It's just the house, dear. Nothing to be frightened about." She hummed to herself. "Oh, I can't wait to see what it has done."

She turned the knob again, and this time the door opened with a *swoosh*.

More gaslights welcomed me, but so did a room with walls painted light blue and gold. A four-poster bed sat in the center. A gauzy canopy hung from the center down toward the mattress. A mahogany dressing table, a changing screen and a deep brown wardrobe all furnished the room.

Winnifred smiled. "I suspect your wardrobe will be full of clothes, too."

It was. Dresses and pants, shirts and blouses all freshly pressed and hanging perfectly greeted me when I opened the doors.

"What is this place?" I said, my voice filled with wonder.

"One of the last places in town still rich with magic. You'll see tomorrow."

Winnifred clapped her hands. "Now. I'm sure Jimmy would've left behind some things. The room will have those for you." She wagged a finger at me. "If you ask nicely, that is."

She laughed a little to herself and plumped her hair. "I'll see you tomorrow morning, nine a.m. sharp at my office."

I stared at the room in fascination. Little gold enameled boxes littered the surfaces. They were delicate and looked to be hundreds of years old. I felt like Belle in the enchanted castle in *Beauty and the Beast*.

I wondered if a candelabra would jump out and start singing and dancing.

I could only hope.

I nodded absently to Winnifred. "I'll see you then."

She stopped before heading out the door to drop the key in my hand. It was solid, weighing a good half pound.

"Guess I won't be losing that anytime soon. It's too heavy."

"That's the only key available now that Jimmy is missing. Please don't lose it."

I clutched it tightly and smiled. "I'll do my best not to."

I escorted her from the house and was about to go upstairs when I noticed a light burning in one of the buildings. The sign hanging above it named the place the Flying Hickory Stick.

It was well-known that Southern witches used hickory trees to make their brooms—the air witches did, at least. The wood was in abundance, light and strong—perfect for flying.

I had no idea what the other elemental witches rode. For all I knew, they grew toads from the ponds and sat on them.

A witch flying over the moon in silhouette was stamped over the Flying Hickory Stick along with a mug of beer.

"Food," I murmured to myself.

15

My stomach grumbled. I stared back up at the room and the loneliness that awaited me there. I could return to it and search for clues about Jimmy, or I could grab a bite to eat and then return to search for Jimmy.

My stomach rolled again, and my problem was solved.

The Flying Hickory Stick it was.

The brass handle felt cool under my touch. I swung the door open and the sound of roaring laughter filled my ears.

The inside was like a tavern—dark wooden furniture abounded and the warm glow of amber light gave a cozy ambience. Booths lined the back wall and each one was bordered with red velvet curtains that could easily be drawn for privacy.

Oh, this was my kind of place.

The laughter that had flooded the room stopped. My gaze swept across the floor, where half a dozen patrons—all men—sat at one table.

Their cold glares felt like ice on my skin. The men stood stock still for a moment, and when one of them moved his arm, he did it with a grace and ease the likes of which no human or witch could mimic.

In that instant I knew I was standing face-to-face with vampires.

Vampires in a town full of witches made absolutely no sense to me. As far as I'd ever learned, the two were mortal enemies. Yet here sat a group of vampires drinking…something in a local tavern.

Deep-rooted fear rose in my chest. Childhood fear, the sort that is ingrained in your brain from an early age. An irrational fear that can't be overcome. It's the boogeyman waiting in your bedroom at night. It's the cold chill of intangible terror, very gripping and real.

I hated vampires but I would not let my first night in this town be ruined by them. I would not bow to my fear and leave the Flying Hickory Stick.

I might not be a great witch, but I was no coward.

I put one foot in front of the other, threw my shoulders back and strode into the den of bloodsuckers.

THREE

*A*s soon as I stepped inside the bar and restaurant, the gazes boring into me shifted back to their own conversations.

I released a deep breath.

"What are you doing here?" came a voice from my left.

I turned to find the bartender polishing glasses. He was a burly man with arms like tree trunks, big meaty fists and a gleaming bald head.

"Um." I cleared the fear from my head. The gaggle of vampires had set me on edge. "I'm new in town."

"Gathered that, ma'am," he said in a smooth Southern drawl. "But why are you here?"

My gaze darted around the dark interior. "I wanted some food. Whatcha got that's good?"

"Pork shoulder sandwich. Fried dill pickle chips. Ranch dressing. Sweet tea."

"I'll take it to go."

He nodded, and before he disappeared into what I assumed to be the kitchen, he pointed a finger at the vampires and said in a threatening tone, "Stay away from them."

I would not be made to feel small and intimidated by a bunch of vampires, so I faced them. But I made sure not to look at them directly. To look at a vampire dead-on was to challenge it.

"What do we have here?" a tall, skinny one wearing Carhart pants, a baseball cap and a white T-shirt said.

Turned out, redneck wasn't just for everyday folks. Looked like this vamp had a good handle on it.

The skinny guy sauntered up to me in a menacing way. I cocked my head. "I am not a *what;* I am a *whom.*"

He swiveled his head back to the crowd. "And *whom* do we have here?" he mocked.

"Not a tasty treat for you," I said defiantly.

He threw his head back and laughed. "Oh, she's got guts, y'all. Walking in here when there's a crowd of vampires. She must either want to be eaten or is spying on us."

Now I might not be the most powerful witch in the world, but if I had to use a bit of water magic to hold him back while I escaped, it could've been done.

The odds were two million, eight hundred thousand, fifty-two to one that I would escape alive.

I would take those odds.

And I would not be intimidated by a vampire living in a witch town.

I smiled tightly. "I'm not interested in spying on y'all. I'm searching for someone."

He cocked a brow. "Oh? And you think we ate him?"

"No," I said stiffly. "I didn't think that until just now. Pretty sure that if you're living in Witch's Forge, then there are rules against you eating any witch here. Am I right? Even me."

The cocky glint in his eyes faded. The table of vampires he had been with stopped talking and started snickering.

Cocky Man opened his mouth to say something when another voice cut him off.

"That's enough, Peek."

Peek? As in peekaboo? I almost laughed out loud. But I was much more interested in discovering who had spoken.

The voice was a rich baritone and filled the room with an authority that made the entire bar stand at attention.

I glanced around and found the body that accompanied the voice standing at the door.

He was tall, athletically built, wearing tan pants, riding boots and a white shirt.

He looked like he'd stepped out of another century.

Well, he was a vampire—I could tell by the slow yet elegant movement of his arm as he slid one hand into his pocket—so he could be as old as time.

He strode over. Dark hair with golden tendrils woven through tumbled over his shoulders. Danger seeped from his every pore. If danger had been a wine, this guy would've been carrying a glass of it.

There was no doubt in my mind he was deadly.

Silvery eyes flashed in the gaslights. What was it with gas lamps? Were they the only means of light in this town?

"I didn't mean nothing," Peek said.

"Ah, grammar at its finest," I murmured.

Anger flashed in the stranger's eyes. He nodded to Peek without taking his icy glare from me. Peek slinked back to the table of vamps.

"You would do well not to insult a vampire," the stranger said in a low voice. It was a warning, but more than that. It was also a threat.

"Your vampires would do well not to insult me."

His lips quirked slightly. I noticed they were well sculpted. In fact, his entire face looked to have been chiseled from stone.

"You're on our territory," he explained.

"I am a witch. This entire town is my territory."

That was as true as I believed it to be. The mayor hadn't told me there were places to avoid. If it had been such a big deal, she would've mentioned it.

Should've mentioned it, at least.

"There are some places witches aren't welcome," he said.

"Then maybe you should put up a bulletin to newcomers and let them know that."

He glared at me, but I would not back down. This vampire couldn't hurt me—not here. Not in public.

"I'm looking for someone. His name is Jimmy. He's about yay high, blond hair—preppy young man. Easy smile. Have you seen him?"

The vampire scratched his chin. It sounded like his fingers were grating over sandpaper as they brushed the stubble.

"I can't say that I have."

I jerked my head to the table. "Maybe one of your cohorts over there has. My friend disappeared. Perhaps they know something about it."

His eyes hardened to the color of flint. "They wouldn't have harmed him."

"They seem so kind and gentle. The type of men who know how to treat a lady with respect."

He scowled. "Like I said, you're on our territory. Witches—reputable ones—don't come here at night."

I gave him a sickly sweet smile. "Vampires, reputable ones, don't threaten witches."

"No." He took a step forward. He was intimidating. I couldn't see one muscle through the shape of his clothing, but there was no doubt in my mind that if he had wanted to, this vampire could've crushed my throat with one hand.

His mouth opened, and a flash of fangs glinted in the light. He was warning me. Maybe I was stupid. Maybe I was full of gumption, high on it, since I had come to Witch's Forge to prove something. Because of that, I would not be intimidated.

Not by anyone. Or *anything*, in this case.

"No," he repeated, "reputable vampires don't threaten witches. We make promises instead."

I opened my mouth for a retort that would've landed me in more hot water when the bartender slapped a bag down on the shiny wooden surface beside me.

"Your food," he said loudly as if to break up the oh-so-amazing conversation the vamp and I were having.

"How much?" I said.

"Five witch's dollars."

I groaned. "I don't have witch's dollars. I have my dollars. American currency." I shot the vampire a dark look. "It's a country that you might not know about since you're probably as old as the dawn of time and who knows how long you've been holed up here."

He smirked. "Quite the attitude."

I rolled my eyes and turned to the barkeep. "Can I pay for it tomorrow? I'll have to get some money."

"Fine." But he added sharply, "Come during the day."

I hooked my fingers through the door handle and glared at the bloodsucker beside me. "Don't worry. I don't have to be told twice."

I moved to leave but heard the vampire's voice behind me. "I didn't catch your name."

I pushed my backside against the door until it gave. When I was halfway out, I replied, "That's because I didn't give it."

With that, I vanished into the night.

Well, not really vanished. I couldn't do that if you paid me. But I did saunter from the bar and back to the house, where I greedily ate my meal atop the lavish bed and then slid under the covers.

But sleep would not come. The image of glowing silver eyes—those belonging to the nameless vampire filled my head and wouldn't leave.

I AWOKE REFRESHED. I checked my phone. No one had called. First things first. I had to track down Jimmy. He would have had a file with the names of folks to match, so I needed to find it. I also needed to know if he would answer his phone.

I dialed his number.

Not sure why I hadn't done that before. I was both horrified and relieved to hear the ringing coming from inside the room.

The sound died before I could pinpoint the location, so I dialed Jimmy again.

I followed the bleating to behind the wardrobe, where I retrieved

Jimmy's cell. I sighed and leaned against the wall, my elbows on my knees.

I stared at the screen. A picture of Jimmy stared back at me, his blue eyes shining.

My stomach twisted. "What happened to you, Jimmy? Where are you? Where is your file?"

The house rumbled and shook. It sounded like something was crawling in the walls. I rose and crouched in the center of the room.

One of the air vents on the floor lifted, and a file spit from the hole and slid across the floor, landing at my feet.

I clutched my heart. "House, you and I need to have a come-to-Jesus. You about scared the life out of me."

The house did not reply.

I picked up the folder and thumbed it open. Inside was Jimmy's calendar. Much of it was blank except for meetings with the mayor, but I noticed in one square Jimmy had written *LH* and *BF*. Hmm.

I peeled back that page and found the completed matchmaking questionnaires for the first couple Jimmy was to help fall in love.

Belinda Ogle, an air witch, and Langdon Huggins, an air wizard, were supposed to have been set up.

I glanced back at the initials—LH and BF. The LH must've stood for Langdon Huggins, but I didn't understand why Jimmy had gotten Belinda's last initial wrong.

Setting that thought aside, I flipped through the documents, but Jimmy hadn't made any notes in the margins. Hmmm. First thing I would do after meeting with the mayor would be to track down Belinda and Langdon, find out what they knew.

My first look at Witch's Forge in daylight made me cringe. The town looked like someone had taken a grime-filled paintbrush and sloshed it over the buildings. Everything was sort of tainted with a dirty hue. The kudzu was more prominent in daylight, snaking around streetlamps, over benches and down buildings.

People milled around, but not very many, and the over-the-top shops looked like they had seen better days. Thick coats of dust covered the windows, and the paint was faded.

An antique shop called Southern Antiquities featured old caul-drons and cast-iron skillets. *That might be interesting to check out.* There was also a magical monogramming shop.

I rolled my eyes. We were definitely in the South. There wasn't much that was bigger than monogramming. If you could place your initials on it, you bought it, even in the human world.

Looked like the witch world wasn't much different.

But what struck me the most was the faded, dirty appearance. Why was Witch's Forge withered up? Why did spells backfire? Why was the magic broken?

I strode over to the mayor's office for answers. She jumped from her chair as soon as I entered.

"Charming!" She reached for me with both hands. Thank goodness it wasn't a hug. "So glad to see you." The mayor turned to a redheaded woman sitting on a chair. Her long tresses were pulled into a ponytail, and she was dressed smartly in a silk blouse and black pencil skirt.

"Charming, this is Emily, my assistant."

Emily rose, wide-eyed and smiling brightly. "Charming, it's so great to meet you. I'm so sorry about Jimmy. He seems like such a good person."

I nodded. "He's a great guy. Did anything seem amiss?"

She shook her head and clasped a hand around my arm. "He was supposed to meet with the mayor, but that was a couple of days ago. I spoke to him the night before, to set up the meeting, but that's the last I heard from him. If I can be of any help, let me know."

"Thank you."

Winnifred gestured toward her office. "Charming, there are some things we need to discuss."

I agree. Like why is your town like this?

I nodded and followed her inside. Her heels clacked all the way to her chair.

I shut the door behind me and settled down. Mayor Winnifred Dixon may have hired me, but I wasn't about to be steered the way she wanted. I laid my elbows on the table and leaned forward.

"What in the world is going on in Witch's Forge? The place is a mess. There's kudzu everywhere. The town looks horrible. What happened here, and why do you think I can save it?"

Winnifred settled back in her chair. She studied me. "Charming, there are some things I need to tell you—things that might explain what happened to Jimmy."

I sucked in my cheeks. "I found his cell. He would never have left without it."

The mayor sighed. She folded her hands in her lap and, without breaking eye contact, said, "Witch's Forge is cursed. I'm afraid Jimmy may have succumbed to that curse and is dead."

FOUR

"Cursed?" I nearly shouted, "More like damned."

She sniffed. "I resent that."

"And you think Jimmy succumbed to it?" Good grief, this just got better and better. I wanted to strangle someone. How could she not have told me before now? Wasn't this something that should've been discussed as soon as I appeared in town—like last night? I might have appreciated knowing that, as well as being informed there was a gang of vampires who took over the local watering hole on a nightly basis.

She patted the air to calm me down. "I don't know for sure. Let me start at the beginning. Witch's Forge used to be a great hub for witches of all kinds. It is one of the few places in the country where you'll find all the elements; therefore, witches used to come here to master their magic. It also worked out that we could be a tourist town."

I wrinkled my nose. "Not anymore."

Winnifred hesitated. "Anyway, yes, within Air Town we have Tornado Hollow, that's where the winds grow—that's for the air witches. In Water Town are the main Enchanted Falls but also a smaller set, also by the same name for the water witches, and then there's Mystic Bluffs in Earth Town for the earth witches and of course Fire Springs for the fire witches. As I'm sure you've guessed, Fire Springs is located in Fire Town.

"All the elements are represented in this area, which is what makes it so special."

"But all that magic should fuel the town, not destroy it," I argued.

"Yes." She paused again. "It should. But about ten years ago is when it started happening. The kudzu started growing, and the grime appeared. Those of us in upper management"—she giggled—"as I like to call it, did the best we could to fight it. We used spells and incantations, magic and whatever we could."

"Ever consider a pail of bleach and a rag?" I said sarcastically.

I mean honestly. This was the problem with magic. In my opinion there wasn't anything rational about it. Growing up, my mother always told me to feel my magic. Let it guide me. What the heck? How could you let a feeling guide a bolt of ice? You couldn't. You needed precision.

So for the inhabitants of this town to think they could kumbaya this problem away was ridiculous.

At least to me.

"We never used bleach, no," Winnifred admitted a little too guilty. "And then the worst started happening—folks left. They just up and abandoned our town."

"Who wants to be attacked by kudzu in the middle of the night?" I muttered.

"Exactly!" She slammed her palm onto her desk. "No one, that's for sure. We did everything we could to keep them, but after a few years people started leaving in droves. Yet it didn't change anything—their power was still broken, even after leaving. Then I got the idea that if we started marrying witches off to each other, people would want to stay. Even if I can't fix everything, I can at least keep folks in my town."

"Which is where I come in," I said.

Winnifred gave me a toothy grin. "Correct. I admit I was a little disappointed that you sent Jimmy and didn't come yourself."

"I'm very busy."

She raised her hands in understanding. "I can appreciate that, and I thought everything was going great with Jimmy until he disappeared. And he was doing wonderfully," she quickly added, "matching an air witch to an air wizard. That's how it's always been done in Witch's Forge—water marries water, earth marries earth...you get the idea."

"But it's not like that in the rest of the world," I said.

Winnifred shrugged. "Our founders wanted to keep the magical lines pure, so marriage within magical elements became the law."

I rubbed my temple. I could feel a migraine coming on. "Has anyone looked into Jimmy's disappearance? Do you have police here?"

Winnifred looked a bit startled at the question. "We don't exactly have what you would call police. Not men in uniform, per se. We have something else."

Did I even want to hear this? From the looks of the town, that something else was probably an army of ants that communicated with antenna signals.

"Okay then. Does that something else know about Jimmy?"

"Yes, they do. As far as I know, it's being looked into."

I sighed. Okay. Well, I'd have to follow up on that. "What about the curse? You said the town is cursed?"

"Oh yes." Winnifred perked up as if I'd given her an injection of caffeine. "Yes, well—that's what we decided. After we couldn't stop the magic from dying, we decided we'd been cursed."

The mayor laced her fingers together and placed them on top of her desk triumphantly.

I glanced around the room as if I'd missed something. "I'm sorry. So, y'all just *decided* the town is cursed because it was the easiest explanation? Is that right?"

"Well, yes."

I licked my lips and prayed for patience. "So there was no evidence. No wizard in the background stirring a cauldron full of malice."

Winnifred chuckled as if that was the most ridiculous thing she'd ever heard. "No, of course not. It was the easiest explanation."

Okay. So I had one missing Jimmy, a possible curse and a collapsing town. Where was I even supposed to start?

Oh! The local authorities. "Tell me about the police, or whatever it is you have in this town."

She laughed nervously. "Funny thing about that."

"Yes?"

"Well," she hesitated. "The beings—I won't say *people*—but the beings who watch over Witch's Forge make sure witches are punished if they break the law. Mind you, people here are generally very good, but sometimes they do get out of line. But anyway, sometimes we have issues and um, the ones who deal with it are—"

I knew what she was going to say before she even finished her sentence.

"Vampires," she said. Red creeped up her throat.

I had no doubt Winnifred Dixon was embarrassed. "What in the world are vampires doing lording over witches?"

It was a travesty. Aside from my own issues with vampires, bloodsuckers and witches hated one another. It was simply in our blood to despise the other. Vampires sucked blood, and sometimes, a really evil vampire would suck a witch's blood in the hopes of gaining some of her powers. There was a vile, horrible history between the two.

Eventually vampires swore never to drink witch's blood and witches swore never to curse a vampire.

It was a tenuous pact and one that I never worried about until I'd stepped into Witch's Forge and realized that a bunch of bloodsuckers were the freaking police.

An old scar on my neck itched. I rubbed the spot where two small puncture wounds had been made and then pushed memories of a dark night from my mind.

"Well, some things happened in the past," Winnifred admitted. "Because of that the joint committee of vampires, witches and other magical beings decided it was best that an impartial group should be sent in. All of the vampires who are here volunteered for their positions."

"And it's a bunch of vampires that keep to themselves, keep folks away from the bar at night and scare the witches."

Her eyes flared with surprise. "You met *him*?"

"I met *them*." I leaned back in my chair. "And they weren't too pleasant. If I didn't know any better, I would say they should be looked at as suspicious characters in Jimmy's disappearance. But now I'm supposed to turn to them for help? No thanks."

"Oh not them," Winnifred said as if that should make me feel better. "Not all of them, just one."

I rolled my eyes. That wasn't any better. "If it isn't all of them, then who is it?"

"Tall vampire, dark hair."

I cringed. I'd met him and been a royal witch to him. "I know who you're talking about."

"His name is Thorne Blackstock."

Of course it was. I cleared my throat. "So if I need to talk about Jimmy, go to him."

She nodded. "He's aware of the situation."

That was funny. When I'd asked Thorne about Jimmy the vampire had said he hadn't seen my friend. So right off the bat, the blood-sucker had lied to me.

I rose. "Good. Where does he work?"

"You mean like an office?" Winnifred said with a tremble in her voice.

"Yes."

"Oh, it's best if you don't visit his office." She laughed nervously. "Going to the police might make you look suspicious."

I rolled my eyes. "How is he supposed to watch over and help if he doesn't have an office?"

"He has an open-door policy at his house."

Great. How medieval could we get? "And this great Thorne allows the peons of Witch's Forge to bow at his vampire feet and ask for scraps?"

"He's not that bad," she said.

29

"He's a vampire. The fact that a town would allow a bloodsucker to be its police is beyond unfathomable."

Winnifred rose. "If it makes you feel better, I believe Thorne is searching for Jimmy."

"It does not make me feel better. I won't feel better until we find my employee. Now. Where does this Thorne live?"

Winnifred didn't look like she wanted to release the information. She clutched her hands and flattened her lips.

"If he has an open-door policy, he won't mind me visiting."

She nodded and explained how to get to his house. I thanked her but, before leaving, had one more question.

"I need to know where to find Belinda Ogle and Langdon Huggins."

Winnifred gave me the directions, which were easy enough—follow Wind Avenue and I'd run into the area of town where the air witches lived.

Lots of segregation in Witch's Forge, it seemed.

I thanked Winnifred and left, thinking about what she had told me.

No, I didn't want to talk to Thorne Blackstock. I'd rather talk to Belinda and Langdon first. I didn't want to have anything to do with a vampire because I despised them.

I hadn't seen a bloodsucker since I was a child.

That was why I hated vampires. I remembered the fear of seeing one—and almost dying at the fangs of a bloodsucker.

FIVE

*M*y phone rang as soon as I hit the pavement. I didn't recognize the number. I paused long enough to place my hand on a building with kudzu covering it.

A vine snapped at my hand, and my skin stung. "Ouch!" I yanked away and noticed a red welt budding. "You bit me, you sneaky vine."

The vine made no reply.

Annoyed and wanting revenge on the kudzu but having no idea how to do that, I moved away and answered the call.

"Hello?"

"Charming, how are you, darling?" My mother's delicate Southern accent drifted through the phone.

Oh, this was going to be fun. "I am just great. You'll never guess where I am."

I couldn't wait to tell her.

"Where is that?"

"Witch's Forge."

The line went silent. "I'm sorry, I thought I heard you say Witch's Forge?"

"I did, Mama. I'm here in Witch's Forge saving the day. And boy, do I understand what you meant when you said this was a dying town. It is in a shambles."

"Is it?" she said without enthusiasm.

"Yeah, it's like the whole place is covered in a layer of dirt. Very weird. Oops, looks like one side of a building just collapsed."

It didn't, but it would irk my mother that I was magicking up soul mates in a town she hated.

"You know, Charming…" I could hear the frantic lilt in her voice. "It doesn't sound very safe there. Perhaps you should leave."

"Nope, not leaving. Too much to do. It's a very needy place. Besides, Jimmy is missing."

"That's terrible, but you don't understand. You really shouldn't be there."

I rolled my eyes. "Mama, just because I'm actually in a magical town that you don't approve of, doesn't give you the right to start telling me where I should and shouldn't be. I'm a grown woman, and in case you haven't noticed, I've been making my way in life by myself for a while now. I appreciate your concern—"

"I'm sending your great-aunt Rose."

I stopped dead. "You wouldn't do that."

"I would. I can't leave Nepal for a few more days, so I won't be there to help you until then."

"*Help me?* What are you talking about?" I clutched my phone. I wanted to throw it across the street but stopped myself. "I don't need your help. I don't need Aunt Rose's help."

"That's enough. I won't hear any arguing, young lady. It's all settled. She should be there in a few hours. Good-bye."

"Dang it!" I growled at the phone and fisted it toward the air. I stopped and looked around. Witches ambling down the street threw me puzzled looks.

Hoisting the phone toward them, I shrugged. "My mother."

That seemed a good enough excuse. They returned to ignoring me.

Great. My mother was coming to Witch's Forge—and so was my aunt.

Awesome.

I slid into my car, cranked the engine and headed down Wind Avenue.

"Let's hope something good happens soon," I grumbled. "Because right now I feel like disappearing the same as Jimmy."

~

THE AIR AREA of town was exactly what I expected. Every wind witch I'd ever met in my life was, to be quite honest, either hippie-dippie or an airhead—no pun intended.

So when I pulled up to a row of cottages topped with wind sails blowing in the breeze, I wasn't surprised.

The kudzu grew here, too, and the trees sagged. They were wilted as if they didn't have enough nutrients. My brows pinched in concern as I inched down the street.

Swirls and ornate lacy carvings covered the homes. Brightly painted swooshes reminiscent of air symbols splashed the sides of cottages, and great colorful sails floated in the breeze, looking like flags dancing in the sky.

A circle of witches practiced yoga beside a fountain. I parked and got out.

The first witch I'd seen, a tall woman with frizzy hair and large, shiny jewelry that covered her earlobes, neck, and wrists, smiled kindly.

"Well hey there. We're so glad to have you here in the wind section of Witch's Forge. Tell me, are you an air witch?"

I squirmed. "I'm Charming Calhoun, the matchmaker."

She blinked at me blankly. "But are you an air witch?"

Ugh. I'd forgotten the prejudice of witches. Witches—all witches, liked to stay with their own kind. "No, I'm a water witch."

Her smile tightened. She automatically didn't like me because I wasn't like her—wasn't an air witch. Even hippy dippies had their issues.

"I'm looking for Belinda Ogle. Do you know where I can find her?"

"I'm Autumn. Come with me."

I followed Autumn past the houses. "So you're the one who the mayor has hired to save our little town."

I rolled my eyes. "So I guess the cat's out of the bag."

She turned, a sly smile on her face. "There's no saving this town by using a matchmaker. It's the stupidest idea I've ever heard."

Autumn walked quickly, and I scrambled to keep up. "Then what do you think the problem is?"

She stopped at a cherry-red door and knocked. "I believe the problem is that the magic is running dry. It's as simple as that."

I'd opened my mouth to question what she could mean when the door opened.

A small woman with wavy dark hair, cocoa-colored skin and large velvety brown eyes greeted us.

"This is Belinda," Autumn said by way of introduction. "Belinda, meet Charming, the new matchmaker."

Belinda took one look at me. Her gaze washed from my head to feet. She opened her mouth to say something and then shook her head and slammed the door.

My gaze darted to Autumn. "What am I missing?"

She laughed and knocked again. "Come on, Belinda. Come meet her."

"I will not. She's going to try to put me with that horrible Langdon again."

I peeled open Jimmy's file and scanned it. On paper, Langdon Huggins appeared to be the perfect soul mate to Belinda.

"Excuse me." I gently brushed past Autumn and rapped on the door. "Miss Ogle, I know you don't know me, but it's my magical system that matched you with Mr. Huggins. It doesn't make mistakes, so I'd like to discuss with you what exactly is wrong."

Silence answered me. After a few seconds the knob turned and the door slowly opened.

Belinda stared at me. "It's your system? Your magic that put us together?"

I smiled widely. "Yes, that's right."

"Then your magic is broken."

Autumn stifled a laugh, and Belinda shut the door again.

I rubbed my temples. This day was already looking like the type that would give me an all-day headache.

I wouldn't be discouraged. I had arrived to do a job, and along with finding Jimmy, I would make a match for Belinda. "Please," I pleaded, knocking on the door. "I want to know what went wrong and if you've seen my employee, Jimmy. You met him."

There was a long pause before Belinda opened the door again. She rested a hand on her hip and eyed me suspiciously. "Yeah, I saw Jimmy. What do you want to know?"

~

BELINDA and I walked through the air section of town. "We capture the wind with the sails," she explained, "and are able to harness it if we need to use our magic. Not that our spells go right. But it makes us feel better to have some magic, even if it is temperamental."

"Impressive." I eyed the brightly colored fabrics waving in the air. "Your area seems to be doing better than the main strip in town."

"Our magic isn't what it used to be. A lot of people have moved, but that still doesn't help their magic." She shrugged. "I guess a lot of folks stay because they figure the devil they know is better than the one they don't."

"Common refrain in life," I murmured. "But you saw Jimmy?"

She nodded. "He told me that he was going to introduce me to the love of my life."

"What did you say?"

"I laughed and said I knew just about everybody in this town—at least the other air wizards. None of them are my match. I know it."

"But air witches stick with air witches," I argued.

We stopped outside a restaurant. Suddenly the door flew open and a man stumbled out.

No, not quite stumbled. It appeared he was kicked from the place. Another man appeared, a grim expression on his face.

"Langdon, I told you to stay out." He swore. "And I mean it!"

The man brushed his hands and disappeared back inside. Langdon, covered in dirt, rolled toward the restaurant. "But you have the best brews," he whined.

"That"—Belinda pointed to the man on the ground—"is Langdon Huggins, the man who's supposed to be my soul mate."

I stared at him and then at Belinda. Frowning, I marched to Langdon and hovered over, inspecting him from head to foot.

He kicked at me. "Get away, lady. I need some space." He lifted his hand, and a slew of witch coins tumbled to the ground. "I've got all this money and nowhere to spend it."

Langdon winked at me. "Unless I can spend it on you. A pretty thang like you probably wants a good time."

He reached for my leg. I wasn't about to let this guy think he could take advantage of me.

I placed my foot on his shoulder and ground down. With contempt in my voice said, "Don't you even think about touching me or any other woman around here. Money can't buy what you want. But you might try sobering up and getting some manners. Now hold still."

I needed to know if Langdon was Belinda's match. I focused on her and, while touching him, turned on the piece of me that held my magic. It was like flipping a switch and hearing a lightbulb buzz to life. As I stared at Langdon, I waited for an image to appear in my head.

That was the crux of my magic. Sometimes, very rarely, I could see matches with my third eye. These soul mates always, one hundred percent of the time, matched the questionnaire.

Except for now. Belinda's image popped into my head, but so did another man's face—and it wasn't Langdon's.

Langdon wasn't her match.

The questionnaire, my mathematically calculated magical system of finding soul mates, had failed me.

It had absolutely failed me.

Either something was wrong with my system, which was impossible, or something was wrong with the way magic worked in Witch's Forge.

No shocker there, right?

I moved away from Langdon and back to Belinda.

She quirked a smug brow at me. "I'm right, aren't I?"

I nodded dumbly. "Yes, you are. You're right. He's not your soul mate."

"That's what I told Jimmy," she said, sounding exasperated. "He insisted, but I told him Langdon was never going to be my soul mate and that he needed to find someone else."

"What did Jimmy say?"

"That he would talk to you."

"Did he say anything else? Like where he would go to search?"

She shook her head. "He mentioned something about Earth Town. Those are the most country bumpkins of us witches. They eat meat and potatoes for every meal—that is, when they're not hunting and killing their food."

Air and earth were opposites to one another and therefore the worst possible match that could be expected between two witches.

"Why would Jimmy go there?" I murmured.

She shrugged. "No clue."

I gave her a brief description of the man I had seen in my vision. "Do you know him?"

Belinda shook her head. "Nope," she said a bit too curtly. "Not at all."

I studied Belinda, trying to decide if she was lying. Figuring there was no way to pry more from her, I simply said, "Thank you. I'll be in touch. There is a match for you—a soul mate—and you're right, it isn't Langdon. It's someone else. I just have to find him."

Belinda nodded. She opened her palm, and a broom that had been leaning against the side of a building rose and flew into her hand.

I gave her a questioning look. "The broom has its own magic," she explained. "It can respond to being called."

The broom was made of a knotted branch that curved at the handle. Twigs were tied to the bottom of it, making it look ancient.

She extended her arm toward me. "This is for you."

I hiked a brow. "A broom?"

Belinda nodded. "It's to sweep out all the cobwebs from your head. To re-examine your magic while you're in Witch's Forge."

"What magic? I barely have any magic at all."

"Take it as you will," she replied. "But it's a gift from me to you—an air witch to a water witch."

As much as I didn't need a broom, I couldn't refuse the gift. It would be rude.

So I thanked her and turned to walk away. The broom zipped from my hand, reared on me and gave me a good solid spank.

"What the...?"

Belinda's laugh floated over to me. "That means it likes you."

I rubbed the sore spot on my tush and glared at the broom. "Come and be good."

The broom zipped into my hand and seemed to settle. I got into my car, stuffed it in the backseat and headed back down Wind Avenue, away from Air Town.

"Jimmy, what were you thinking? Why have you disappeared?"

I was heading somewhere that would hopefully help me find those answers—Earth Town.

SIX

*B*ut first I decided to stop back at the "house" for a change of clothing. I use the term "house" loosely because, after all, it did look like a county seat courthouse.

I'd just unlocked the door when a *swoosh* of magic billowed beside me.

I groaned. My mom had not been kidding when she said she would send Aunt Rose. Talking with my aunt was like being stuck in a *Golden Girls* episode.

"Charming," she said in her most exasperated voice, "I thought you'd never arrive. I was about to melt in this heat."

As much as I didn't want to, I slowly pivoted my body to face Aunt Rose.

Her curly white hair was perfectly fixed, her dark sunglasses were perched on her head and her baby-pink dress suit was immaculately pressed. She looked spectacular for her sixty-plus years.

If only her mind was as perky.

"Aunt Rose!" I threw my arms around her. "I'm so happy to see you."

If there was one thing about Southerners, it was that it was most polite to lie. You could be having your arm amputated, and if someone asked how you were doing, the best answer was, *Fine. I'm doing just fine.*

And you couldn't forget to ask them how they were. Because otherwise would be rude.

Rose squeezed me. "I came as quickly as I could."

The smell of White Shoulders drifted from her skin. My great-aunt loved her old lady perfume. It was one thing she took from the nonmagical world.

She straightened her arms and drank me in with her gaze. "You look well, dear, but I was so worried when your mother told me where you were. I thought for sure the curse on this place was going to rub off on you, make it so that you started losing your power, too."

I smirked. "I'm only visiting. I'm not sure it works like that." I nodded toward the house. "Would you like to come inside?"

She fanned herself. "Oh yes, it's sweltering out here. I assumed that block of ice I stuck up my skirt would keep me cool, but it hasn't worked yet."

I swallowed the giggle threatening to overtake me. "Block of ice?"

Rose literally pulled a Rubik's Cube–sized block of ice from her suit and dropped it into the bushes. "I'll have to figure out what I did wrong with that spell," she murmured.

I glanced around to make sure no one had seen my aunt's embarrassing motion. Luckily no one gaped at us.

I led her in. Rose took one look at the staircase and blank walls on either side, fisted her hands to her hips and said in a commanding voice, "This won't do at all, house. I need a bedroom, and I expect a kitchen downstairs as well—fully stocked."

My jaw dropped as the house unfurled like a bow. A hallway unrolled like a tongue on either side of the staircase.

Beside me, a wall popped. A dark oak door with a crystal knob appeared. Two more doors sprang up on the other side, both appearing after a good *pop* and wall rumbling.

The house creaked and groaned as if it were stretching itself to the very edges of its capability. I swear wood splintered and concrete cracked, but when the house settled and the dust cleared, there was a parlor, kitchen with a dining room and an extra bedroom.

Rose brushed her hands. "Much better. I don't know how the house expected you to live completely upstairs. Not with your old aunt here with you. Besides, in a few days your mother will arrive and a new room'll be added on then as well." She shouted up the stairs. "Do you hear me, house? You'll have to make more room soon. Don't be so stingy."

She shook her head at me. "I swear these magical buildings think they own the place. Well if it wasn't for witches and wizards, they wouldn't exist. Much less be able to add rooms. Mind of their own. Of course, the house may have actually stolen a witch's mind in order to be made."

"What?"

She nodded. "That's how they used to do it in the old days—make magical buildings. So barbaric." Rose smiled widely. "But don't worry, no one's going to steal your mind, Charming."

Relief flooded me. "Great."

She considered it for a moment. "At least, I don't think so. But you never know. It is possible, I suppose."

I fanned myself. "Whew. Is it hot in here or what?"

"Yes, I need a change of clothes."

My aunt spun around and changed into a linen blouse and pants. "That's good, but I could use something to shade me from the sun."

Rose pointed to her head, and a safari hat complete with mosquito netting capped her crown.

"Too much?" I asked.

"Oh, Charming," she said, all doe-eyed, "you can never be too careful when it comes to your skin. Ever. It's always good to take care of it."

She smiled wide, inhaled deep and said, "Now. What's going on here at Witch's Forge?"

"One of my employees is missing, and I just tried to match a witch with her soul mate"—I held out the folder in frustration—"but discovered that the man my magically mathematically perfect spell had matched her with was wrong. *Wrong*."

Now that I thought about it, the entire situation was horrible. "It's completely wrong. Which is impossible. That spell has never been wrong before. Why would it suddenly be wrong now?"

I fisted my hands in frustration. Here I was trying to prove to my mother I could save a town, but the entire foundation of my plan was crumbling.

Why would that spell, which was always right, suddenly be wrong in Witch's Forge? Outside magic wasn't supposed to be affected in this town. But maybe it was.

"It's because of the way magic works, or is *broken* here, I suppose," Rose replied breezily.

I shot her a confused look.

"While I can't read minds, I can read expressions. Come to the kitchen. Let's have a nice glass of sweet tea and talk about it."

While I watched, Rose started the tea. With one wave of her finger, the faucet turned on and a tendril of magic erupted from the spout. The line of water coiled around a cabinet handle and started opening and closing doors until it found a pot. The finger of water curled around the handle, dropped the pot on the stove, poured part of itself into the mouth and then turned the burner on. It then went about finding a box of tea leaves and dumping them in.

"Not too much tea," Rose said sharply. "I swear it's so hard to find good help. I once had a finger of water that insisted on trying to brush my teeth at night."

I hiked a brow. "Doesn't sound so bad."

"It is when you're asleep. The thing would wake me up trying to shove a toothbrush in my mouth. It wouldn't have been so bad except I always had my retainer in my mouth, too. Can you imagine trying to brush plastic? It was ridiculous."

"So what'd you do?"

"Well, I did whatever you do when you need to get rid of something—took the water into the forest and lost it."

I nearly died laughing. The idea that my aunt would traipse

through the woods with a finger of water and then throw a stick and tell it to fetch while she ran in the other direction was an image.

As my laughter settled and I admired the humor in Rose, I was reminded of another, less humorous person in my life.

"Why doesn't my mother want me here?"

Rose opened her eyes wide. "In this house? I have no idea."

"Not the house—Witch's Forge."

"I don't know. Why don't we have a nice glass of tea and sit quietly for a few minutes?"

I shot her a hard look. "You're hiding something. What?"

"Nothing." She stared at the pot. "Oh look. Tea's done."

"Already?"

She shrugged. "I might've helped it out." Rose made a glass of sweet tea and placed it in front of me. "Looks delicious, but it could use a shot of bourbon."

I quirked a brow. "The tea?"

"No." She pointed to the water that was still hanging out above the sink. "That. It needs to, as you kids say, chill."

"What is it about this place?" I said.

Rose mumbled something under her breath.

I leaned forward. "What was that? I didn't catch what you said."

"I said it may have something to do with the"—she hid her mouth behind her hand—"prumphemcy."

"The what?"

"The prumphemcy," she mumbled.

"You're going to have to speak up. What does it have to do with?"

"The prophecy, for goodness' sake." Rose flexed her fingers in anguish. "Your mother doesn't want you here because of the prophecy that the swamp witch gave. That witch was high from eating an entire bowl of boiled peanuts—I told your mother not to offer them because they always made the witch give silly prophecies. Why, there was this one time the swamp witch prophesied that an entire honeysuckle bush would try to devour the town we lived in—Magnolia Cove."

I quirked a brow. "Did the bush try to do that?"

"No. Well, it tried, but apparently ended up with an upset stomach after eating its first chimney, so it gave up."

I had to clamp my lips shut and call bullcrap on that one. "What prophecy?"

"I already told you, the honeysuckle—"

"Not that one," I nearly shouted.

See? This was why my aunt irked the heck out of me. Trying to have an actual conversation with her was like banging my head repeatedly against a brick wall.

I didn't even have to hit my head to suffer brain damage around Rose. Just trying to converse was damaging enough.

"Oh, well, it was a prophecy that you'd, um—really, I probably shouldn't say."

"Cat's out of the bag now." I smirked. "Why not just go ahead and tell me? Then we can make our way over to Earth Town or a vampire's house, to see if he's awake and ask him if he's found my friend."

She gasped. "A vampire? Dear, if a vampire's found your friend, he's probably sucked him dry."

I slapped my thigh. "That's what I think, too, but the mayor is unconvinced. This vampire is apparently the town's law enforcement."

Rose's eyes widened in that doe-eyed look again. "If he's the law, we should talk to him, don't you think?"

"I'd rather not," I muttered.

But Rose had jumped on that train of thought like a tick on a dog. "If we want to find your friend, we'd better see that vampire." Rose clapped her hands, and the arm of water grabbed her glass of sweet tea.

When it reached for mine, I pulled it away from its grasp. "I'm not finished hearing about the prophecy."

Rose's gaze narrowed. "Didn't you come to Witch's Forge to find your friend?"

I hiked a shoulder. "Well, when you put it that way, it makes me sound petty to want to hear a prophecy."

"Not petty, just misguided." Rose hooked her purse on her arm. "But if you must know, you'll lose your power."

The information hit me like a ton of bats. "What?" Then I thought about it. It wasn't like I had a world of power to begin with. I shrugged. "Whatever. I don't care. Might as well use it as long as I have it, huh?"

Maybe I could still save this town.

Rose nodded. "I'm so glad that went well. I was worried you'd be all upset."

I shrugged. "I'm already a disappointment to my mother. This won't matter."

Rose shot me a sympathetic look. "Okay. I'm ready to talk to the vampire with you. Which way do we go?"

I sucked down the rest of my tea and rose. "Let's get in the car. I think we should be able to find the place."

I strode from the kitchen. Rose followed, heels clacking. "Oh? What makes you say that?"

I glanced over my shoulder and smirked. "Because apparently he owns a house the size of a castle."

"In the Smokies?" The shock was not hidden in her voice.

I nodded. "Yep."

Rose threw back her shoulders. "Well, what are we waiting for? Let's go find a vampire."

SEVEN

*T*all and wide, made of stone and towering at least four stories, Thorne's house looked more castle than home. A wall of trees hid the house from passing vehicles.

Rose and I sat in the car for a moment while I collected myself.

"What are you doing with a broom made of sticks?" Rose asked.

"Oh, an air witch gave it to me."

"Why?"

I shrugged. "She said it would sweep out the cobwebs in my head. I don't know. Perhaps she thought my house needed tidying up."

"Did she see your house?"

"No."

"Did you tell her it was dirty?"

"No."

Rose sighed. "Then I don't think that's why she gave it to you."

"Well, why did she then?"

"I don't know. Let's go."

A few moments later we stood at the manor's front steps. I didn't know what to call it other than a manor. I could've called it a castle because it pretty much looked like one, but I didn't want to give the vampire that much credit.

I knocked and said absently in reply to Rose's question, "I don't know why I have the broom. Belinda reached out her hand, the broom came to her and she handed it to me. Maybe that's how they pay people in Air Town—with brooms."

I shrugged. "That's probably it. She thought I needed payment for matching her, and that's what the broom was for."

Rose sniffed. "Seems like an awfully cheap gift, if you ask me."

"I wasn't."

"Don't worry, I won't tell your mother that you're being bribed by the local townspeople."

"With brooms, no less." I rolled my eyes. "When is someone going to answer this door?"

The door swung open as if on command, and there stood Thorne himself, wearing jeans and a button-down plaid shirt. His hair was tied back. The vampire almost looked human.

Too bad his silvery gaze on my face made my stomach turn.

"Hello." I smiled brightly even though my gut twisted at the sight of him. "I don't believe we officially met yesterday when your friend was harassing me, but I'm Charming Calhoun. I've been hired by Mayor Winnifred Dixon to save Witch's Forge from—um, itself, I suppose."

He hiked a dark brow. "The matchmaker?"

The tone in his voice suggested Thorne didn't believe love, or even matchmaking, could save much of anything. I cleared my throat and widened my smile. "That's me."

"How do you do?" he said in a voice as smooth as chocolate looked velvety in a television commercial. You know the kind, where the chocolate is all melted and someone's dipping a whisk in to make it rich and creamy before it gets poured into a chocolate mold, packaged and shipped to your nearest grocery store.

Yep, that's what his voice sounded like. I swallowed a knot in the back of my throat and pushed all that away.

"I'm doing very well, thank you. This is my Aunt Rose."

His gaze slashed to her. Thorne extended his hand like a gentleman. Rose fitted hers inside, and he kissed it.

47

What the...? Why didn't he kiss my hand?

Not that I wanted him to. His touch was probably cold—like the undead are, cold and lifeless. His lips probably felt like fish lips on her skin. I'm sure Rose would want to vomit after letting a vampire touch her.

I sneaked a glance over my shoulder.

My aunt beamed at the bloodsucker.

Traitor.

"May we come in?" I said. "There's a matter I need to discuss with you."

Thorne stepped back graciously. "Please. By all means."

Y'all, the place was grand, and I don't mean because it was large. Yes, it was large with a tall, almost cathedral-like ceiling. Dark wooden furniture was sprinkled about and covered in plush, colorful cushions. Gold clocks sat on surfaces alongside antique vases. Ancient rugs lined the floors and portraits with gilded frames hung on the walls.

I didn't want to ask, but I had a feeling that most of his collection was older than I was—way older.

Without a word Thorne led us into a sitting room replete with a monstrous mantel that a person could've stepped into.

Thorne asked if we would like something to drink. Rose, taken by her surroundings, replied, "No, but I would sure love to meet your decorator. They have taste."

I cringed. Thorne smiled. "I did most of this myself. After having it shipped here, of course."

I sat in a horsehair chair he motioned to, and Rose did the same. "We took a risk by coming during the day. I didn't know if the stories about vampires and daylight are true."

"They are not," he said without a hint of tension in his voice.

I'm sure he got that a lot—people wanting to know about vampires and him having to repeatedly explain what they were really like.

It was probably very annoying.

I thought this as he studied me with those silver eyes. A flush crept up my neck. I glanced away and could've kicked myself for it.

I did not want to appear weak in front of a man whose cronies had been real jerks.

"I'm sorry for my friend's behavior last night."

Could he read my mind? Maybe. I didn't know what sort of powers vampires actually had. If he could be awake during the day, could he also guess what I had for breakfast?

"Tell me about that," I said.

He smirked. "He is…they are…territorial."

"The bartender told me not to return at night to that pub."

"What pub?" Rose asked.

"The one in town."

Thorne brushed lint from his jeans. "It's not a place for people at night."

I bristled at his statement, that a witch couldn't enter a business at night, but I decided to ignore it and move on. "The mayor says you're the local sheriff." I laced my fingers together and hooked them over one knee. "I have to admit I was shocked to hear that vampires were lording over witches."

Anger flashed in his eyes. "First of all, we don't *lord* over anyone. But yes, if there's a problem, I look into it."

"You? Not those men?"

"Me."

"Then what are those other vampires here for?"

"That's none of your concern."

"One of them almost ate me."

Rose gasped. "He did?"

He jabbed his finger into the leather armchair. "You were some-place you shouldn't have been."

I rolled my eyes. "Why don't you go ahead and blame the victim, then."

Thorne's voice hardened. He spoke so modern, as if Jim Halpert, sarcasm and all, had just landed in Witch's Forge. "If you knew a street was dangerous, filled with thieves, but you chose to walk down it late one night, who do you have to blame when you end up robbed?"

"Oh, yourself," Rose said eagerly. "Definitely."

I shot her a scorching look. "That's not the point, Rose," I said through clenched teeth.

"Well it is, if the nice Thorne says so. You'd do best to leave that pub well enough alone." She gave me a motherly pat. "Besides, what's a nice girl like you doing in such a place late at night? People might talk. They might wonder what their matchmaker is doing in there."

I clenched my fists. "Okay. I get it. Stay away from the gang of vampires who, for some reason that I can't know, hang out in a witch town."

Thorne nodded. "Precisely."

Infuriated by what he *wasn't* telling me, I changed topics. "A couple of nights ago my employee went missing." I pulled Jimmy's phone from my pocket and flashed his picture. "Last night, why didn't you tell me that you've seen him?"

Thorne studied the screenshot. "Because I haven't, not in the flesh. Though I've been looking for him."

I frowned so deeply I felt a fissure forming in my forehead. "If you haven't seen him in person does that mean you've seen him in the blood?"

Thorne's smiled tightened like a tug-of-war rope. "Miss—is it *Miss*? Or do you have the privilege of torturing a significant other?"

I glared at him. "It's Ms."

"Ah." He threw his head back in mock appreciation. "Ms. Calhoun, I'm well aware your employee is missing. I've been searching for him ever since Mayor Dixon told me he'd vanished. The problem is"—he leaned forward, whispering—"I haven't found him, and no one seems to have any clues to his whereabouts."

"This," I said, "is his phone. Found it where I'm staying."

"I searched there." He drummed his fingers on the arm of his chair. "The house neglected to give it to me."

"And what else have you missed?" I said, testy. I raised my palm. "Wait. Don't answer that. You wouldn't know what you've missed because you wouldn't know you've missed it."

His gaze could've scorched the hair from my head.

"Did you search Earth Town? Apparently he said he was going there."

Thorne nodded. "Didn't find a trace of him."

"Maybe he went home," Rose offered gently.

I had to stop myself from snapping at her. "Without his phone? No. Jimmy is an exceptional employee. He wouldn't disappear without a trace. He'd let someone know."

Thorne laced his fingers together and studied me. "So Jimmy didn't tell you anything?"

I hedged. "He left a message a few days ago that something was wrong. But I didn't receive it until yesterday."

Thorne extended his palm. "May I hear it?"

I swallowed nervously but managed to retrieve my phone and play the message for him.

"When Mayor Dixon called and said she thought something had happened to him, I came here. And what I've found is distressing—a phone that's still charged and a vampire leading the investigation."

His razor-sharp jaw tightened. The light splashing across his face made me take in his features clearly for the first time—high cheekbones, eyes that could cut glass with the sharpest of glances, and a nose that was fairly straight but looked like it might've been broken at one time—before he became a vampire, no doubt.

He eyed me coolly. "You don't like my kind. But that's okay. May I have his phone so that I can study it for clues?"

I dropped it hard in his hand. "Is it that obvious that I don't like you?" I said sarcastically. "I don't understand why a vampire would want anything to do with a town of witches—a broken town at that— unless you're here to pick us off one by one."

Anger flared in his gaze. Thorne averted his glance to a spot on the floor. When he spoke, it was slow and deliberate.

"Ms. Calhoun, I would appreciate it if you left."

I clicked my tongue and shook my head. Just when the going got tough, the vampire couldn't take a little heat.

Rose tugged on my sleeve. "Dear, I believe this nice gentleman is asking us to leave."

No one said anything. Silence filled the room. Seeing as I wasn't going to get any more out of the bloodsucker, I rose, determined to find Jimmy myself.

He didn't care about my friend. He didn't care about anything except his band of merry vampire men.

I followed Rose from the room. A wind slashed past us, and by the time we reached the door, Thorne was standing there, his gaze pinned on me.

Flames rose in my cheeks. I wouldn't be bested by a vampire. No way.

I shot him a challenging look and then turned up my nose and walked past him.

"Good day, Ms. Calhoun."

"Mr. Blackstock," I said.

"I never introduced myself."

"You didn't have to," I explained smugly. "I already knew who you were."

Without another word he shut the door. Rose and I walked silently down the steps toward my car.

When we reached it, she turned to me. "Wow. Did you feel that sexual tension back there? I'm sweating."

A jolt flared down my spine. "What are you talking about?"

Rose fanned her hand in front of her face. "The way he was looking at me. If I were twenty years younger, I'm pretty sure the two of us would've had to leave you and get a room."

I pinned my lips together and nodded. "Yep. The two of y'all had some real sexual tension. You should watch out. He is a vampire."

We slid into our seats, and Rose buckled her belt. "He might be a vampire," she mused, "but I have the feeling he's soft as a kitten once you get to know him."

I gritted my teeth. "I would rather light my hair on fire and run naked through town than get to know a vampire. No thanks. The last thing I will ever do is become friends with him."

And that was a promise.

EIGHT

Since Jimmy had been planning on going to Earth Town, I talked Rose into visiting the area. We didn't get there until after the sun had set and dinner had passed, which I figured was safe from vampires since they hung out at the pub at night.

Drinking what? I didn't know.

Earth Town was much more spread out than Air Town. The houses were situated farther apart, leaving room for large gardens to be planted on open tracks of land.

"What are earth witches like?" I said to Rose.

"Oh, they're more in touch with the ground and nature than a lot of us. They tend to grow vegetables and such. Salt-of-the-earth sort of folks."

Up ahead, a pavilion sparkled with life. Christmas lights dangled from the rafters, and a group of folks all dressed in plaid shirts and either jeans or blue-jean skirts headed toward it.

"What's going on?"

Rose giggled with excitement. "I would guess that's a good old-fashioned hoedown."

My jaw dropped. "A hoedown?"

"Also known as a hootenanny or a jamboree. But that's only if I had to guess. Roll down the windows and let's see."

I paused. Every fiber in my being resisted the idea of a hoedown, hootenanny or jamboree. These things were not of my world. I was a high-heels-and-concrete-jungle sort of gal. Not the kind that threw on plaid, yanked on a pair of cowgirl boots and put on a straw hat.

The window buzzed as Rose rolled it down. "Well, since you're not going to do it," she murmured.

The sounds of a violin wafted into the car.

"A violin?"

"In this case it's called a fiddle."

"Whatever," I murmured.

"Pull over. Someone here may have known Jimmy."

I shot her an are-you-kidding look. "You're joking, right?"

Rose's face lit up. "Come on. Let's go dance. I haven't been to a good old-fashioned jamboree since I was at least twenty. It was so much fun. I ended up with mud in my hair and maybe a few kisses that I won't tell you about."

I nodded. "Sounds about right. I don't want to know about them."

I parked and we got out, following the flood of folks to the pavilion. The music roared to a quick pace while men and women took to center stage. The outside was lined with haystacks, of course, because you couldn't have a hootenanny without hay, obviously.

Men and women stood side by side. With their arms locked, they started shuffling their feet.

Rose clapped to the music. "That's square dancing," she shouted to me.

You'd never know it was a dwindling town with these witches. They were throwing their heads back, laughing and being merry.

I felt like an idiot dressed in my linen shirt and slacks. Like a sore thumb.

Which may have been why a pert little blonde wearing her plaid shirt cinched at her belly button and a pair of cutoff shorts that nearly exposed a butt cheek zeroed in on me and headed over.

Her blonde hair was pulled into a high ponytail reminiscent of *I Dream of Genie,* and blue eyeshadow smeared her lids.

She smacked her lips. "You're the new matchmaker, ain't ya?"

I nodded. "Charming Calhoun."

The woman grasped my hand and pumped it up and down. "I'm Kimberly Peterson, and I'm dying to find my soul mate. Can you help me? Please!"

"May—"

I was going to say *maybe,* but Kimberly cut me off. "All I ask is that he's tall, rich, hysterical and likes horses. Sort of like if you could find a cross between Paul Bunyan and Prince Harry, that would be perfect."

I gestured to the dancers. "Is that man in here?"

"Of course he ain't." She fisted a hand sassy-like to her hips. "If he was, I would've already met him and married him. I would've made sure of that."

Ah. So Kimberly was what I would call *aggressive* and *possibly desperate.*

Two scents males could smell from a mile away.

She would be nearly impossible to match.

Rose shouldered between us. "Young lady, what's going on here?"

Kimberly became even more perky, if that was possible. Her eyes flared, and she got a lilt in her voice. "Oh, that's our summer hootenanny. We do it every year as our way to thank the goddess for the last year's harvest and to ask for plentiful crops this year."

"I'm surprised your crops still grow," I commented.

Kimberly nodded. "Soil doesn't require magic."

My gaze snagged on a man with auburn hair and striking light eyes. I gripped Kimberly's arm.

"What is it?"

I pointed to him, not wanting to take my gaze away in case he disappeared. "Who is that man?"

Kimberly turned to see who I was pointing at. "Which one?"

"The one with the hot dance moves, slim hips and big shoulders—red hair."

She rolled her eyes. "Oh, that's Cap Turner. Every girl wants him, but he's sworn off women."

"Why's that?" I said.

"Said he's leaving town the next train that comes through, which is a laugh since the train hasn't run in years. But anyway, Cap's gonna find himself an earth witch who likes adventure."

"He doesn't need an earth witch," I murmured.

"Of course he does." Kimberly threw back her head and laughed. "Every witch knows you stick with your kind. That's how it is."

I shook my head. "I've got just the witch for Cap, and her powers don't come from the earth."

Kimberly frowned. "Oh? Where do they come from?"

But I was already off, darting through the crowd, hoping to catch Cap as soon as the song was over. I doubt Kimberly heard my response, and even if she did, I doubt she would have believed me when I said Cap needed an air witch.

Because his was the face I'd seen with Belinda. I wondered if Jimmy had seen him, too.

No chance of finding that out until I found Jimmy, though.

The song ended, and Cap turned to leave the pavilion. I caught up with him as his booted feet hit the hay-covered floor.

"Hi there," I said, beaming.

Cap looked me up and down. "Do I know you?"

I thrust out my hand. "I'm Charming Calhoun. The mayor hired me as the town's official matchmaker."

Cap shook my hand but stared at me vacantly. "Oh. Well, I hope you do well."

He started to brush past me, but I held my hand up to stop him. "I have someone I'd like for you to meet."

Cap raked his fingers through his hair and shot me a lopsided grin. "Ma'am, I appreciate you taking an interest in me, but I can say with all honesty in my heart that I am not interested in whatever it is you're selling."

"I'm not selling anything," I stammered. "There's someone I'd like for you to—"

"Get your hands off me!"

The crowd quieted and turned in the direction of the sound. Langdon, the drunk I'd originally had pegged to match with Belinda, threw out his hand toward an earth wizard.

"You need to calm down," the man said.

Langdon, drunk and belligerent, shoved him away. "I said, get your hands off me!"

"Excuse me, ma'am." Cap moved toward Langdon, facing him down. "I told you to stay away from here, Langdon. You're nothing but trouble."

Langdon's face reddened to nearly burnt. "I ain't talking to you! You always mess things up, Cap. I came here once and for all to tell you to stay away from my girl."

I frowned. What girl? Could Cap know Belinda?

"You need to stop talking while you're ahead, Langdon," Cap said.

Langdon growled like a feral wolf and rushed Cap. Cap dodged sideways and chopped the air, hitting Langdon between the shoulder blades.

Langdon fell to the ground with a *thump*. He whimpered but didn't get up. I suppose he was too drunk to lift himself.

Cap moved to him. "I'll get him out of here."

Some of the elder men nodded at Cap, glaring at him as if this was all his fault.

With Cap heaving Langdon away, I moved back to Rose and Kimberly.

I turned to our newfound friend. "What was that all about?"

Kimberly *tsked*. She waited until the music started back up before replying. "Langdon wants this air witch, Belinda, to be with him, but she won't have anything to do with that drunk. Now, it's not absolute fact, but it's rumored that a couple of years ago Belinda and Cap had a thing but broke it off because they couldn't be together."

"Because of their opposing magic," I said.

Kimberly nodded. "Everyone knows it's bad for witches to mix." She leaned in and whispered, "They'd have children born without magic, and then the town would die."

I nibbled the inside of my lip as I considered it. "But this town's already dying."

"But it isn't completely dead," Rose said, flabbergasted. "I suppose a little more suffering couldn't hurt anything, now could it?"

I shot her a confused look. "What does that mean?"

"I mean, maybe a little love couldn't make things worse. How could it when there's already a coat of magical grime on the town—the sort of sludge that only appears when the magic is broken. When something's off."

"Here in the outskirts, I don't see anything off about it."

Rose and Kimberly exchanged a look. "I'll show you," Kimberly said.

She disappeared into the night and didn't reappear for several minutes. When she did, she brought back a watermelon. It was the size of an orange.

"Is this a watermelon?" I said.

She nodded. "Fully formed."

"Oh, this is bad." I cocked a brow at her. "I thought you said soil doesn't need magic."

"Things grow, but not like they should. Used to the melons would double or grow fat as ticks on a dog's back."

"Ew," I said. Some visuals I simply didn't need. I didn't need to think of a fat tick about to burst from sucking blood. Reminded me too much of vampires.

One vampire in particular.

Not because he was tall, had muscular shoulders and was incredibly attractive. That had nothing to do with it. This was because he was nasty and sucked blood. Plain and simple.

"Then why are your people staying?"

It seemed a reasonable question. Kimberly nibbled her bottom lip before answering.

"I guess 'cause we're loyal to this place—to this land. We've lived here for generations. Generations upon generations of earth witches married earth wizards here, and continued the family line."

"Well I can understand that." Rose smiled kindly. "In my family we all lived in the same house until it got so old it started crumbling. My ma would put magical bandages on it, but after a while the bandages lost their stickiness. Didn't hold anymore."

Kimberly frowned at Rose, and I wanted to shrink and disappear. I mean, there was no such thing as magical bandages for homes, I was pretty sure.

Was there?

"Charming! I'm so glad you decided to come out and meet some of the locals."

I glanced up to see Mayor Dixon and Emily marching toward us.

"Mayor Dixon." I greeted her with a smile and a handshake. "My aunt and I came out to see some of the local color."

"Oh yes." The mayor flicked her fingers toward the pavilion. "Hoe-down night is one of my favorites. It's a wonderful summer tradition." She leaned over and whispered conspiratorially, "Usually there's a little bit of love in the air as well. If I had to guess, I'd say that's why you were here."

"I hope the townsfolk have been behaving themselves," Emily said smartly. "We walked up when one of them was being rowdy."

Kimberly rolled her eyes. "You know that's just how Langdon is. He gets drunk and angry and then someone has to throw him out of wherever he happens to be. Ain't nothin' new about that." She nodded to me. "Except Charming here has promised to introduce me to a rich man."

I frowned. "I never said that."

After all, I was still pondering how my matchmaking question-naire could've put Belinda and Langdon together in the first place. But now I realized her true soul mate was Cap, an earth wizard.

And unfortunately, Cap didn't want to talk to me.

My gaze flickered to my watch. "Well, it's been nice talking to y'all, but I think it's time for us to head out."

We parted ways, but Kimberly made me promise before I left that I would give her the questionnaire. It wasn't a problem, really. After all, I was supposed to match folks to keep them in this town. It was all part of the job.

Rose and I were heading back to the car when strange lights appeared out in a field. They looked like lightning bugs but were the wrong color—they were iridescent blue.

"What are those?" I said.

Rose clutched my shoulder. "Those are critter bugs."

I shot her a skeptical look.

"No, they really are. They're called critter bugs."

I unlocked the doors. "I've never seen them before."

"Of course you haven't. I mean, I guess I'm not surprised you haven't before. It's not often anyone sees them."

I started to get into the car and stopped because Rose stood stiff, staring at the critter bugs.

I sighed. "Okay. Why don't people see them often?"

"Because," Rose said quietly, "critter bugs only appear at night when they're hovering over a dead human body."

A jolt ran all the way to my toes. "What did you say?"

Rose slowly turned to me. "Critter bugs clean things up. They eat dead flesh."

"So you're saying?"

Rose pointed toward the lights. "There's a dead body out there in that field."

I slammed the door. My first thoughts were of Jimmy. I prayed it wasn't him. "What are we waiting for? Let's see what sort of dead body it is."

NINE

I pulled my phone from my pocket and used it as a
flashlight. I'd love to say I was such an awesome witch that
I could make a light ball form in the palm of my hand, but that was
a lie.

Rose could, even though she was a water witch.

"Your man-made devices aren't nearly as good as the originals."

She snapped her fingers, and a ball of light zipped out in front of
us, lighting the way.

"Do you have to be such a show-off?"

My aunt plumped her hair innocently. "It's not my fault your
mother used up all the magic in our family."

I smirked but said nothing because it was true, and my mother had
said that a thousand times.

We reached the flurry of critter bugs. When they saw us, they flit-
tered away. They hovered in the recesses of our light, waiting for us to
leave so they could return.

I flashed my phone on the ground.

There, in the middle of the grass, lay a man. I held my breath as my
light washed from his feet to his head.

I released it when I realized the dead man wasn't Jimmy.

It was Langdon Huggins. I nearly vomited when I saw what had killed him.

It looked like Langdon's chest had been ripped to shreds.

In the time between Langdon's outburst at the pavilion and now, something or someone had murdered him.

"We need to call the authorities," I said. "And get the mayor back here. Now."

~

COUNT DRACULA SHOWED up about five minutes after the mayor alerted him.

"And what made you come out to this field again?" he asked me, his voice dripping with contempt.

"Critter bugs," I explained.

He quirked a brow. I sighed and shook my head in annoyance. "My aunt explained that critter bugs hover around dead bodies. I guess they eat the flesh, but you wouldn't know anything about that, would you?"

Thorne's silvery eyes narrowed. "Then what happened?"

"Then we came out here and found Langdon dead, and me, being the responsible person I am, made sure someone contacted you, the local vampire, since you're apparently in charge of murders and missing persons. How're things going with finding Jimmy?"

He ignored my question. Oh, the cockiness of this man was so annoying.

Thorne knelt down. He washed a hand over the body. "The area around him has been trampled." His eyes glittered with accusation. "Did you do this?"

I shook my head. "No, I didn't walk all around him to see if he was dead." I pointed toward Langdon's lacerated body. "It's pretty obvious."

He whirled on me. "You didn't see who?"

I shook my head. "If that had been the case, I would've given you their name, don't you think?"

"Unless you were protecting them."

I fumed. "I'm not protecting anyone. In case you hadn't noticed, I'm not the person with a band of angry, sullen vampires at my heels."

Just then the voice of Peek, the nasty vampire who'd threatened me before, rang out. "What have you discovered, Thorne?"

I scoffed. "See? A whole bunch of vampires doing witch's business."

Thorne rose. Flecks of anger filled his eyes. "For your information, those vampires help me. They help this town with crimes. All of them do, and the reason they were so particularly rude to you last night was maybe because you were fresh blood walking into a den of vampires doing business. Did you ever stop to think of that?"

"No, and I don't want to. I want to find my friend—a friend who had contact with this dead man only a few days ago. Maybe there's a connection." I slapped my thigh in frustration. "Heck, half the town knew this guy was a drunk. In one day I watched him get thrown out of two places."

Interest flared in Thorne's eyes. "Where was the first?"

"Air Town."

Thorne's gaze flickered to his vampire cohorts. "Find out if anyone here is an air witch."

The vampires quickly dispersed, and good riddance to them. One bloodsucker was bad enough. I didn't need to be surrounded by a whole flurry of them.

I bent over Langdon's body and stared at it. Something long and wiry stuck out of his shirt pocket.

I plucked it out. "What is this?"

"That could be evidence," Thorne snarled. He bent down to see what I had taken.

I raised the wire into the moonlight and quickly realized it wasn't a wire at all. "It's a hair. A really long, kind of gross hair."

It *was* gross—about six inches and thick, which was why I had originally thought it was a wire.

Thorne snapped open an evidence bag. "Would you please stop touching evidence?" He plucked the hair from my hand and dropped it in the bag.

"Thank you."

"Wow. So polite."

He bristled. Like literally, Thorne's back bowed. "For your information, I'm generally very polite, but only to women who actually have charm as opposed to simply being named 'charmed.'"

"Oh, haha."

He rose. "I'll be in touch if I find your man, Jimmy. Now it's time you went home and left the investigating to the investigators."

Thorne turned away from me, effectively dismissing me like I was a child.

I gritted my teeth and walked back to the car, where Rose was waiting.

"Did the vampire ask about me?" she said, fluffing her hair.

"No. But he certainly thinks he knows it all. Except when it comes to Jimmy. He isn't helping."

We slid into our seats. I stared through the windshield, irked that he'd dismissed me so easily.

After firing up the engine I turned to Rose. "I tell you what, there's something I don't trust about that vampire."

"Oh, there is?"

"Yep, and I plan to find out what it is he's hiding."

WHEN WE REACHED the house that night, I went upstairs to my room and stared at the walls. "There has to be more about Jimmy that I'm missing. Is there something else? House, do you have anything else? Did Jimmy have a journal or leave a slip of paper somewhere?"

The house was still for a moment; then it coughed and churned, clanged and rattled.

The door flew open, and Rose stood there, cold cream covering her face and her hair tied up in a scarf.

"What in the devil is going on? Did you ask the house to change for you?"

I shook my head. "No, I didn't. I only asked if Jimmy had left anything else."

She clutched my vanity, trying to hang on while the structure rumbled. "Well, it sounds like the house is looking to cough up Jimmy along with half a lung."

"Let's hope not," I murmured.

But it turned out Rose was closer to being right than I was. After what sounded like a coughing fit met with a bunch of burps, the transom above my door opened and something fell out, landing on the floor.

I shot Rose a confused look. "What in the world could that be?"

Rose quickly recovered the object. "It's a shirt."

I lifted the arm. "And not just that. It's been torn. Ripped."

Sure enough, Jimmy's favorite striped shirt was ripped in the back. It looked like someone had pushed the thing through a cheese grater.

"Does Jimmy normally rip his clothes?" Rose asked. "As sort of a way to punish himself?"

I had no idea what she was talking about. "What?"

"You know. Like self-flagellation. When people whip themselves. I mean, come on. That's what it looks like. That your friend likes to rip his clothing."

I shook my head. "I don't think Jimmy would've done that. Those look either like knife marks or claw marks."

At the mention of claws, Rose and I exchanged a charged look.

"You don't think—" I started.

"That we could be dealing with more than a disappearance?"

"Why else would his clothes have been ripped?"

Rose poked the air with authority. "Unless someone wanted us to find this—his ripped shirt." She shook her head. "Charming, I don't know, but it looks like we're dealing with more than a simple disappearance. It looks like either Jimmy ripped right out of his shirt or someone ripped it off him."

I grimaced. "It's too bad this house can't talk."

"Oh, I know." Rose nodded in understanding. "Think of all the mice it would tell us run around at night. Not something I want to have on my mind when I'm trying to go to bed."

I nearly slapped my forehead. "That's not what I mean."

Rose couldn't hide her surprise. "It isn't?"

"No. What I mean is, whatever happened to Jimmy started here. His disappearance. All of it. It started in this house." I balled up the shirt into my fist. "That's why it gave us this. But what we need to know is who could've caused this, and the one person who knows everyone in town has an office half a block away."

"Who?" Rose asked.

I narrowed my gaze. "The mayor. I'll be talking to her first thing in the morning."

TEN

"*I* need to know who could've done this." I lifted the shredded shirt over the mayor's desk.

Winnifred Dixon's eyes widened in surprise. "What is that?"

"It's my employee Jimmy's shirt. It's been ripped to shreds."

Fear shone in her eyes. "Is there...is there blood on it?"

"No blood."

She sighed with relief. "Thank goodness. This town has enough problems. We don't need another possible murder investigation."

I dropped the shirt onto her desk. "Listen, Mayor. You invited me and my people into your town. Now my man is missing and his shirt is shredded. This looks like the work of a creature that's not a witch."

"You mean a vampire," Emily, the mayor's assistant, offered.

"Emily," Mayor Dixon reprimanded. "That's unnecessary."

"But it's true," I said. "What other creature could leave claw marks like that?"

"But there's no blood," the mayor argued. "If Jimmy had been wearing the shirt when he was attacked, then surely he would've been scratched."

"Unless he wriggled out of it in time," I argued. "Now. You've got a vampire running around who thinks he owns the place. He's the only creature around here who could've done it."

"Done what?"

I hadn't heard the door open. But the voice that asked the question was new. It was just my luck that I'd be caught talking about the one creature in town who could walk soundlessly into a room.

But I wasn't intimidated by Thorne with those razor-sharp eyes, high cheekbones and pecs that probably meant he could bench press a whale. I had nothing to fear from a vampire in a Podunk town.

I turned, brandishing the shirt. The flash of his silvery eyes caught me off guard, but I shoved my visceral response aside. "Could've done this."

His brow quirked in mock surprise. "And you think I got angry and shredded a shirt? You seem to think I don't have anything else to do."

My jaw dropped. Why was he being so difficult? "This is Jimmy's shirt. I found it in the courthouse. Jimmy wouldn't have destroyed it, and I didn't. I don't know many witches with claws that could shred something like this." I poked his chest. "But you could. Ouch. You're really hard."

He shot me a smirk of superiority that I wanted to smack right off his face. "With my fangs, I suppose. Shred it, I mean."

"Absolutely."

He crossed his arms and leaned his slim hips on the lip of the mayor's desk. "So let me get this straight—I went into a bloodthirsty rage and tore into your friend's shirt, obviously without him in it because if I had managed to rip it while your friend was wearing it, there would've been blood everywhere."

"You're making fun of me."

He cocked his head. "I'm suggesting you keep to what you know best—matchmaking—and let me do my job."

"What? Lord over a town of defenseless witches?"

"You're hardly defenseless. And my job is none of your business." His gaze shifted to the mayor. Clearly he was done with me and our frivolous conversation. "I'm going to bring in a suspect today. I want you to be there for questioning."

"For the murder last night?" I said, butting in.

He dragged his gaze from Mayor Dixon and glared at me with disdain. "This is none of your business. I would appreciate it if you excused yourself and went about your matchmaking."

I gritted my teeth. "There's no need to concern yourself with my missing friend, Mr. Thorne. I'll find him myself."

With that, I turned and stormed from the office. Jimmy's shirt slipped from my fingers and fell to the floor, right in front of Thorne.

I moved to snatch it, but the vampire was faster.

Of course he was.

He held the shirt for me to take. I stared at him, not making one move.

He leaned over and whispered in my ear. "What's the matter? Afraid I'll bite?" In that moment I was acutely aware of his breath tickling my ear. That he smelled of grass after a rain with a touch of vanilla and musk.

Something stirred in my gut.

I narrowed my eyes and threw my head back so that he faced me. "The last thing I am is afraid of you."

I snatched the shirt from him and left the office, stomping out to my car.

I STOOD in the middle of the street, unsure of what to do next. Rose was back at the house, probably cooking breakfast for us.

I had a shredded shirt but no idea what to do with it. I also had two witches from very different backgrounds to somehow get together, but I was still working on a plan for that. All these things were drifting through my head when a semi-familiar voice rang out.

"Is that you, Charming?"

I turned around to see Kimberly Peterson waving her pink-painted nails at me. She smiled brightly, and I had the feeling this woman might be more trouble than she was worth.

But on the other hand, I was supposed to bring all the soul mates in Witch's Forge together, so I might as well set about doing it.

I smiled brightly. "Hey, Kimberly."

"Hey." She beamed. "I was just wondering if you had time to find my soul mate because I just know he's out there somewhere. I know that once we're together and he makes my dreams come true, I'll be the happiest woman in the world. I just know it."

"Come with me."

"Where to?"

"I don't have any of my papers here. I have them at the place I'm staying. We'll do it there."

Kimberly clapped her hands with glee. "Oh, goody. Now I'm not crazy about going into the old courthouse, what with the fact that the place has a mind of its own, but I really want to know my future."

She grabbed my arm as if panic had taken hold of her. "When you do a match, is it forever? Does it last for all eternity? Until death and all that?"

I nodded. "So far."

I opened the courthouse door and stepped inside. Kudzu had started creeping onto the walls. They hadn't bitten me yet, but I wasn't putting anything past them. I shuddered. The last thing I wanted to be living in was a building filled with bugs and vines.

"Charming, are you back?" Rose called from the kitchen. "I've got fresh sausage and biscuits."

"Yes, I'll be there in few minutes."

Rose stuck her head out of the kitchen door. She spotted Kimberly. "Oh, we have a visitor."

"You don't mind me," Kimberly said. "I'm going to have my soul mate found. I won't be but just a minute."

Rose waved a spatula. "You take all the time you need. I'll keep breakfast warm."

I led Kimberly to my room.

"Wow," she said. "This is like a princess's palace."

I laughed. "I know. I was waiting for the silver hairbrush to start talking, but it hasn't yet."

Kimberly smirked. "You never know. Give it a few minutes and maybe it'll at least dance."

That was when I realized that even though Kimberly was boy crazy, I liked her. She was funny and seemed to be nice. It couldn't hurt to have a friend in town.

"Now, tell me about my true love. He'll make all my problems go away."

Okay, so maybe I needed a friend who was a touch less delusional. Meeting a man wasn't going to make any of your problems disappear. In fact, it might make them worse.

Sure, if you were dating a serial killer.

But I didn't match serial killers. My magic didn't work that way.

I pulled a slip of paper out from my briefcase. "This is my magical matching questionnaire."

Kimberly stared at it, a blank expression on her face. "I don't see any questions."

I smiled mischievously. "It doesn't have any. All the questions are magically built in. When you press your hand to it, that's when the magic starts to work. Are you ready?"

She looked hesitant. It was strange, I knew. I wasn't using any sort of mind tricks to find matches, I was using plain and simple magical math—the best kind of magic, if you asked me.

A second later Kimberly flattened her hand on the page. Tendrils of magic curled up from her hand. Sparkles flared on the paper.

I clapped. I couldn't help it. I always got excited when someone had a match.

"You have a soul mate! You can take your hand away."

Kimberly pulled it away. Words dappled the page. The questionnaire, as I called it, wasn't exactly a questionnaire; it was more of a sponge that soaked up the person's personality and displayed it in words and phrases.

Words like *courageous* and *loyal* dotted the sheet in all different sizes and scripts. Some of the words were written from left to right, while others were written top to bottom, like a crossword.

But at the very bottom squatted four little words that made all the difference. "You have been matched."

"Is his name on there?"

I hid the sheet from her because I wasn't trusting the names that were appearing—Langdon Huggins was case and point. I wanted to see for myself.

I closed my eyes. That was when I saw him.

"He's tall, dark and handsome."

Kimberly clapped. "I knew it."

I let the image fill my mind. "He looks rugged yet refined."

"I'm loving this more and more. What's his name?"

I hedged. "I don't have a name."

Kimberly stuck out her bottom lip and pouted. "That's too bad."

But smoke filled the image behind the man I saw. It rose high, billowing up. When it cleared, I noticed a wheel and steel.

"Witch's Forge has a train station, right?"

Kimberly stared at me. "Yes, but like I said, it hasn't run in years."

"That's where he's going to come from. The train."

Kimberly hooked her purse onto her shoulder. "Well then, what am I doing around here? I have to make sure I get that train station up and running."

She darted out the door before I had a chance to say anything else.

"Well," I said to the empty room, "I suppose if anyone has the will to get a train station up and running, it's that girl."

I was about to sink onto the mattress when I remembered Rose had breakfast waiting for me.

I filed Kimberly's sheet away and tromped downstairs.

"Your vampire didn't care about the shredded shirt," I shouted out to Rose from the hallway. I reached the bottom floor and headed into the kitchen, fully expecting to see my aunt standing by the stove, her spatula still in hand. "I think it's suspicious and we need to snoop—"

I stopped. Sitting at the table was a tall witch with fiery red hair and bone-white skin. Her soft pink dress practically flowed like water down to the floor, even seeming to puddle at her feet.

Leave it to my mother to dress like an angel but have the personality of a succubus.

I meant that nicely.

Mama rose. "Charming," she cooed, flowing over to me and kissing the air beside both my cheeks. "I left Nepal and came as soon as I could. This place is horrible. I thought Witch's Forge couldn't get any worse, but it seems to be crumbling all around us."

As if on cue, a loud crash came from outside. "See? That was probably the building across the street falling to its death. Darling, we've got to get you out of here as soon as possible. This isn't the place for you. In fact, I'm afraid that if you stay here, your already limited magic will burn out and die like everything else."

I smirked. "I know why you're here, Mama."

Panic filled her aqua eyes. "You do?"

"Rose told me about the prophecy."

My mother shot Rose a dark look. "She did, did she?"

I nodded. "Yes. I know I'll lose my power. That some swamp witch eating boiled peanuts told you that."

My mother's gaze pinned on Rose for a moment. Rose shrugged innocently. "Is that right?" Mama said.

I folded my arms. "To be honest, I don't understand why you'd be so worried about it. You already say I don't have much power to begin with. Why would you care if I lost it?"

Hurt filled my mother's eyes. "It's true you're not nearly as good a witch as I am, but I want you to keep whatever power you have."

"If that's the truth and you want me to succeed, then I know a way you can do it."

Her eyes hardened. "Charming, are you brokering a deal with me?"

"I am." I smiled coyly. "If you want to get me out of Witch's Forge, all you have to do is one thing."

"And what would that be?"

She would hate it. My mother would absolutely despise what I was going to ask. She'd rather burst into flames than stay in this hick town any longer than she had to.

"Help me find Jimmy."

I fully expected her to say no. To run out the door as quickly as possible.

Instead, my mother smiled widely. "Why, I'd love to help. What should we do first?"

ELEVEN

*W*hat happened next was exactly what I expected. As soon as my mother stepped outside in her flowing pink dress, coupled with her long red hair and the fact that she carried herself like the Queen of Sheba, she was surrounded by a throng of people.

"Are you Glinda Calhoun?" said a sad-looking witch with dark circles under her eyes and frizzy blonde curls.

My mother threaded her fingers together and placed them beside her chin. She tipped her head to the side, plastered on her biggest smile and said, "Why yes, I am. What can I do for you, dear? Besides fixing your hair and making you as beautiful as me, that is?"

I rolled my eyes. My mother believed the entire world needed fixing. She believed beauty made the planet a better place and it was her job to help others—however they needed.

"Tell us how you saved the children of South America from that army of ants."

A gaggle of folks had arrived by now, enchanted with my mother's beauty and ability.

"Gather round," she said, "and I'll do more than that. I'll teach you how to use magic to help yourselves."

I rolled my eyes.

"Looks like she's got an audience," Rose said.

I nodded. "She'll forget all about us. I'm heading out. If you want to stay with Glinda the Good Witch, go for it."

Rose looked torn. "I'm coming with you. Your mother can take care of herself."

We slipped away, leaving my mother in her natural element—as the center of attention. I don't even think she noticed we'd disappeared.

We arrived in Earth Town a few minutes later. It didn't take long for me to find out where Cap lived—on a farm not far from the pavilion.

I arrived just as Cap was staring at a hay bale. He scratched his head. Rose and I sat in the car watching.

"Think he's trying to work some magic on it?" Rose said.

I hiked a shoulder. "No telling. Let's go find out."

We approached. My heels wobbled on the gravel driveway. I had to walk slowly to keep myself from falling over. Ugh. What I wouldn't give to get out of this place and return to civilization—where I could get a decent cup of coffee for five bucks and feel the beautiful hardness of concrete underneath my two-hundred-dollar pumps.

"Cap," I said pleasantly, "I don't think we had a chance to really talk last night. I'm Charming Calhoun."

He scrubbed a hand over the stubble on his chin. "I remember," he said without a hint of interest.

I laughed nervously. I hated it when I had to approach folks who were absolutely not interested in talking to me. It made my job so much harder.

"I understand you used to be involved with Belinda Ogle."

"What's it to you?"

I rubbed my lips together. "I was wondering why you broke up."

"Why do you care?"

"Because I've been hired to fix this place. Fix Witch's Forge, and the way I'm doing that is by bringing witches and wizards together."

"Seems like enough witches and wizards are together. I don't see how that's going to save the magic in this town. Look at my hay."

I stared at the yellow ball of grass. "What about it?"

"Whatever's taken hold of the center of town is out here, killing the soil in these fields. Won't be long now before we won't be able to grow anything. We'll all have to leave, abandon this place."

"That's what I'm trying to stop. I need your help. Look, I'll tell you straight. Langdon and Belinda were matched to be together."

"I heard." He raked his fingers through his hair. "I don't see it. That guy was nothing but an alcoholic. When she wouldn't have him, he thought it was my fault."

I cleared my throat. "Why would he think that?"

"'Cause Belinda and I were together in high school. Then we broke up."

Cap turned away. "Look, I've got work to do. I don't have time to discuss my private life with some stranger."

"Is that a potbellied pig?" Rose pointed to a little pink pig with a dark spot over one eye. The swine ate slop from a trough. "I just love potbellied pigs. Can I hold her?"

For the first time Cap smiled. "Sure you want to get your clothes dirty?"

Rose dismissed his concern with a wave. "Oh, I'll be able to clean up just fine. There's nothing better than feeling a baby pig's tongue licking your face."

"I would disagree," I murmured.

Cap plucked the pig from the pen and settled it in Rose's arms. I swear my aunt squealed like a pig with joy.

"Oh Charming, you've got to hold her."

"No." I didn't hesitate. "Are you kidding? I'm not holding a pig. I would rather walk through a pit of rattlesnakes than touch that dirty animal."

Cap's eyes widened in astonishment.

I cringed. Okay, maybe I shouldn't insult the man I wanted information from.

"I just mean I'm a city girl," I said quickly. "I don't know anything about the country. I barely like dogs or cats, much less a pig."

The creature's mud-caked feet pawed the air. There was probably poop on them.

"Swine are one of the cleanest animals around." Rose cooed to the pig. "You are clean, aren't you, precious?"

I nearly vomited.

"Besides," my aunt continued, "if you hold the pig, you might find out other things you want to know."

She nodded at Cap. Realization slammed into me. Oh my gosh, she was right.

When I saw the look of appreciation that filled Cap's eyes as he watched Rose holding the piglet, I realized this was my only way in. In order to get this man to talk to me, I would have to hug a pig —literally.

Heck, at least I didn't have to kiss it.

The things I would do for my job. I cringed, wanting to run the other way, yet I managed to extend my arms, reaching for the creature.

Rose placed the squirming animal in my arms. Sure enough, the pig licked my cheek. It was wet, but I managed not to grimace too much.

"She sure does like you," Cap said. "She's squealing up a storm."

"Oh, that's great," I murmured, trying to keep the pig from climbing all over my face. "She's sweet."

"You should keep her."

I balked. "I'm sorry?"

"You should keep her. The pig. She loves you."

"I don't need a pig."

"Sure you do, Charming," Rose said, butting her nose in my business. "Who doesn't need a pig?"

"I live in a condo. I don't think they allow pigs as pets."

Rose peered over my shoulder and shot kissy faces to the pig. "You never know until you ask. Besides, I think Cap would like it a lot if he knew this little gal was taken care of."

My gaze flickered back to Cap. He smiled proudly at the sight of the pig in my arms.

I rubbed my lips together. An idea was forming in my head. "Okay. I'll keep her, but you have to answer some questions."

He raked the back of his hand down his cheek. "Shoot."

Yes! I was in. "What happened between you and Belinda? Why'd you break up?"

Darkness smeared his face, but as quickly as it formed, it vanished. "We were told by our parents we couldn't be together. She's an air witch, and I'm an earth wizard. Everyone around here knows the only way we keep this town going is by making sure we stick to our own kind."

I nodded. "Each element stays within its tribe."

Cap stared at his hay bale. "Right. So we were forced to break up."

"Oh, that's so sad," Rose said. "It's like Romeo and Juliet. Except you didn't kill yourselves. At least not yet."

I shot her a dark look. "It isn't anything like that."

"Well sure it is," she said. "They're told by their parents they don't belong together, but then against all odds they make sure they are allowed to love each other."

"They broke up," I said through gritted teeth.

She shrugged. "Well then it's almost like Romeo and Juliet."

I sighed, knowing I wouldn't win this argument. "So your parents kept you apart."

Anguish filled his eyes. "That's right."

If I could convince Cap that he was supposed to be with Belinda, I would make my first match in this town.

I stared at the sad-looking hay bale. "So everyone in this town is supposed to marry a witch of their kind. Does anyone ever depart from that rule?"

Cap shook his head. "No way. We keep to it. That's how it's been ever since Witch's Forge was created."

"Is it a rule?"

Cap nodded. "Written in the town's charter. Witches intermingling makes bad stuff happen."

I frowned. "What sort of bad stuff?"

Cap thought about it for a second and then hiked a shoulder. "I don't know. The old folks always said bad stuff."

"The town would lose its power," Rose answered.

I scoffed. "Town's already losing that. That can't be the reason."

Rose *tsked*. "You never know, Charming. A town losing its magic is a bad thing. I mean, look at those sad hay bales. That should be golden brown. Instead it's just brown. It won't be long before no one will be left in Witch's Forge."

It all started to make sense. Now that I knew the town had outlawed witches with different powers to marry, I was beginning to see what was going on.

"Cap, thank you for talking to me. I have a question for you—if the town changed the law and you could be with Belinda, would you do it? Would you date her?"

Cap rubbed the back of his neck shyly. "Well, I don't know, Miss Calhoun. That's a lot to think about."

I grabbed his shirt collar. "I don't need you to think about it too much, Cap. I'm offering you to be able to date your high school sweetheart. The girl you wanted to date before your parents got in the way. Would you do it?"

Hesitation flashed in his eyes.

"For goodness' sake, assume I'm not going to tell that vampire police officer and get you arrested. Just tell me straight."

Cap nodded slowly. "Yep, I'd date her."

"Great." I moved to leave and remembered my manners. "Thank you, Cap. I'll take good care of the pig. Do you have a name for her yet?"

"No name. Y'all can come up with that."

I smiled to him and turned away, handing the pig to Rose. "You're in charge of her. I don't have time for a pig."

Rose beamed at her. "They're just the cutest, Charming." Rose snapped her fingers, and a bar of chocolate appeared in her palm. She shoved it under the pig's nose.

The pig opened her mouth and swallowed the chocolate whole.

"Is that good for pigs? Chocolate?"

Rose patted her head. "It'll be fine. You're going to love having her."

I frowned. "I doubt it. Listen, I'm going to drop you off at the house. I've got some things to do."

"What things?"

I started the engine and gripped the steering wheel until my knuckles whitened. "First, I have to get that stupid law changed."

"What else?"

"I still don't trust that vampire. Of all the creatures who could've ripped Jimmy's shirt, I think he's the prime suspect."

I shifted the car into drive and peeled down the gravel road, kicking up rocks and dirt along the way.

I gritted my teeth. "That vamp is hiding something, and I plan to find out what."

TWELVE

I dropped Rose off with Pig and noticed my mother was still sitting in the center of town, a large crowd surrounding her.

"And that's when I learned that you can mix fire magic and ice magic, though the results can be unstable," she said.

The crowd oohed and ahhed as she demonstrated. Even though my mother was a water witch by nature, she could tap into a little bit of fire magic.

One of her favorite things was to show off about it.

I rolled my eyes and entered the mayor's office.

The first thing I heard upon entering was the sound of coughing, or rather hacking. It sounded like a cat trying to lung up a fur ball.

"Mayor Dixon?" I said hesitantly.

No reply. My heels clacked as I walked to the back of the office, where I found Emily standing over a trash bin.

That awful hacking continued until Emily saw me. She put the trash bin down and stopped. She wiped her mouth and said sheepishly, "Sorry. Something went down the wrong pipe."

"Sounded like you were spitting up a fur ball," I joked.

She brushed her hands down her silk blouse and smiled. "What can I do for you, Miss Calhoun?"

"I'm looking for the mayor."

"Oh, once she heard Glinda Calhoun was giving magic lessons, she headed out to listen."

I groaned. I'd obviously overlooked her in the crowd. *Great.* It would be impossible to drag her away from my mother. No one ever wanted to stop listening once Glinda Calhoun got on the storytelling bandwagon.

The door to the office opened, and the mayor's voice drifted in. "You know, you should really give an official talk here. We would love to advertise that Witch's Forge is hosting the great Glinda Calhoun in a one-night-only event. Folks would come from nearby states to hear what you have to say."

I watched as my mother followed Winnifred Dixon into the office.

The mayor continued. "You could possibly attract a whole new generation of folks to settle here. It would be wonderful."

"Thank you, Mayor," my mother said coolly. "But I'm only in town to visit my daughter." Mama's eyes flared when she saw me. "And there she is. Where did you get off to, Charming?"

"I didn't think you'd noticed," I muttered.

An uncomfortable laugh trilled from my mother's throat. "Of course I noticed, pumpkin. I'm your mother. I notice when you run off."

Mayor Dixon sat in her chair and circled around. "Your mother gave the most fabulous discussion on magical theory."

I twirled my finger. "Whoop dee do. Did she tell you all her greatest victories? How she created the wall of water and made an army of trolls think the earth had split in two?"

"Yes," Winnifred said in wonder. "She even explained how water magic is the most fluid of all magics."

I raked my fingers through my hair. "They're all fluid—well, maybe not earth, but the others are fluid. Anything built on feelings like that is fluid and slippery. Magic is all touchy-feely stuff."

"But not your magic," my mother said sharply. "It's all mathematical and scientific. Starched-collar sort of stuff."

"My magic works just fine," I argued.

"What you have of it," she countered.

I glared at her. This was the same argument we had over and over. My mother put down my magic, and I scoffed at hers. It never changed.

"Why did you come?" I said.

My mother ignored me. "Mayor, it was wonderful meeting you. I'll consider your proposal. Charming, I'll see you back at the, ur, house?"

"Sure."

She practically floated from the office. Once my mother vanished out the door, I turned to the mayor.

"Mayor, there's something we need to discuss."

A dreamy expression filled her eyes. She stared off in the distance, and I knew Winnifred was fantasizing about hosting my mother in an event and then all the people would see Witch's Forge—a grimy town overrun with vines.

Yeah, folks would want to stay here.

Not.

"Mayor, I need you to change the law that witches of different powers can't marry."

The mayor blinked at me. "I'm sorry?"

"I need you to change that law."

"Why?"

Here went nothing. "Because I think that law is killing this town."

She scoffed. "Nonsense. That law is what keeps the balance in Witch's Forge. It's been like that for years. Besides, everyone knows that if witches of different magics marry and have children, those children will be born without powers. They will be sterile. That would kill the town."

I shook my head, but she continued, "The power within us is what keeps the town magical."

"But your magic doesn't work. It makes sense that sooner or later babies will be born without any magical ability, if you keep to your theory."

"None have been born so far," she said proudly.

"But that doesn't mean it won't happen." I sighed heavily and clasped my hands. "Mayor, you hired me to fix this town by marrying folks. The magic in this town is beginning to affect even my work. When Jimmy made the initial match of Belinda Ogle and Langdon Huggins, it appeared right on paper—each had the other's name stamped on the bottom—but when I met with Belinda and used my magic to see her match, it wasn't Langdon. In fact, it was a wizard in a completely different magical clan."

The mayor gasped. "It must be wrong."

"It isn't wrong. My magic isn't. Not about this."

The mayor flicked her hand at me. "Then move on to another person. Find a match where the two witches are in the same magical town—a Fire Town witch and a Fire Town wizard."

I sank into a chair. "Don't you think that if two folks from the same town were going to be soul mates, they would already know each other and be together?"

The mayor's cheeks burned bright red. I had her there. "I can't go changing that law. Witches wouldn't know what to do with themselves."

I cocked my head. "Is that what you really think? I want to save Witch's Forge. But to do that, I need your help."

"Changing the law won't help."

I tapped my fingers on the desk. "Tell you what. If I can prove to you that the law needs to be changed, will you do it?"

She stared at me for a moment. "Perhaps."

I glared at her.

Mayor Dixon swallowed loudly. "Yes, okay. I'll propose we change it. But you'll have to create a miracle if you want me to make that happen. It's hard to get folks to change their ways."

I rose. "You know, Mayor, if there's one thing I've learned while finding people's soul mates, it's that when love is in bloom, people are more than happy to change things about themselves. It may not be permanent, but they'll change nonetheless. I think you'll also find that the younger generation, those who are ready to get married, would be more than happy to see the law revised."

The mayor eyed me skeptically. "You may be right, Charming, but I still need proof."

I walked to the front door and turned around before exiting. Emily entered from the back office. I nodded to them both.

"Then proof is what I'll get you."

WHEN I REACHED THE HOUSE, Pig was running around the kitchen, squealing like a, well, pig.

Rose laughed. She was slicing up vegetables for the pig to eat while feeding her chocolate kisses on the side. My mother was nowhere to be seen.

"Where's Mama?"

"Oh, she's inspecting the house, trying to get the darned thing to create her bedroom just the way she wants it."

I rolled my eyes. "And here I thought this was going to be a short visit."

My mother's voice drifted in from the doorway. "I'm staying as long as you are, Charming, so you might as well figure out how to get along with me."

My gaze darted to her. She flicked a long tendril of red hair over her shoulder and smiled smugly.

"I know you're joking. You're the one who always puts down my abilities."

My mother scoffed. "I don't put down your abilities. I love what little magic you can do. You're very talented at your little match-making thingie."

I shook my head at Rose. "See? She just put me down."

"It did sound that way, Glinda." Rose dropped another chocolate into the pig's mouth. She grunted with pleasure. "I'm sure that's not how you meant it."

"It is," I protested. "It's how she meant it. My little powers are no match for hers."

"My dear, you've never even attempted to use more of your powers."

"That's not true. Remember when I tried to make it snow?"

My mother sauntered into the room and plucked a radish slice from the cutting board. "Yes, I remember. You tried, poor dear." Her teeth crunched into the vegetable. "Some of us just have different talents."

"Like math and science," I said snidely.

"Exactly."

I shook my head in frustration. I did not come to Witch's Forge to have a come-to-Jesus discussion with my mother. I preferred when she was in Nepal, attempting to save the world instead of me.

I didn't need saving. I was doing just fine, thank you very much.

I also didn't need to have my mother nagging me, and me yelling at her for nagging me. Or for following me around, as it was.

I sliced my hands through the air. "For now, let's call a truce."

My mother blinked at me blankly. "I was never waging war."

"Oh me neither," Rose blurted out. "The last thing we need in this town is a war. Can you imagine—all that kudzu exploding and more grime covering the streets?" She shuddered. "Why, it's enough to want to take this little potbellied pig and go live in a tent in the wilderness."

She considered that. "Granted, the tent would need running water and a bathroom. Probably a mosquito fogger, too. Oh, and a bed for Sweetie Pie to sleep in."

I cocked a brow. "Is that what you're naming the pig? Sweetie Pie?"

Rose laughed. "Oh no, that's what I call my handsome lover who visits me once a month."

I raised my hand in a stop gesture. "That's enough." I turned to my mother. "I call a truce. I won't pick at you, and you won't pick at me."

"Wonderful." Mama smiled. She tapped a finger on the table, and a crystal glass filled with ice, tea and lemon slices appeared. "Want one?"

I couldn't tell if she was goading me or not. Mama knew I couldn't work that kind of magic. But since I'd called a truce, I'd better stand by it.

"Sure."

She magicked me a glass and I sat.

"Now," she said authoritatively, "let's get down to business. What's going on with Jimmy's disappearance?"

My eyes flared. "You want to help me?"

She tossed her hair over one shoulder and said, her voice dripping with spite, "Really, Charming, you act like I'm the enemy."

"Sometimes you act like that," I said barely above a whisper.

She shot me a look that could've fried me on the spot and sipped her tea. "What's going on with it?"

I got her up-to-date on what I'd learned so far, minus my theory about why the town's magic was broken—or cursed, if you wanted to believe the mayor.

"And that shredded shirt, where'd you get it?" she asked after thinking about it for a few minutes.

"The house gave it to me. But not right away. For some reason the structure kept hold of it."

She scoffed. "These old magical homes are particular. Sometimes you have to be specific in what you ask for. Other times the house will give you everything plus the kitchen sink when all you wanted was a toothbrush. I agree, it's peculiar."

"Not as peculiar as the vampire police," Rose said.

My mother cocked a brow at that. She hated vampires almost as much as I did. "Vampire police? That's a new one."

I nodded. "Yes, and out of all the people in this town, a vampire would have the strength to shred the shirt barehanded. I have the feeling the vampire chief is hiding something."

My mother smiled. "Vampires are dangerous."

The gleam in her eye told me where Mama was going with this. "They are, and if I was looking for clues about Jimmy, I bet we might find something at the chief's house."

"It's risky," she said. "We should leave that to the police—oh wait, he's the police."

My mother rose with a flourish. Her skirts dusted the floor in a romantic, almost gothic sort of way.

She downed the rest of her tea and stared at us. "Well, what are we waiting for? It's about to be dark, and if we're going to break into the vampire's house, we'd better start planning how to do it."

"Break in?" Rose said, flustered. "We're going to break in like common criminals?"

My mother shook her head. "I prefer not to talk so commonly about the situation. And bring the pig. We're going to need some help with this."

THIRTEEN

The manor, as I had started referring to it in my head, was
quiet. Almost too quiet.

Rose, my mother, the pig and myself sat in the bushes about a
hundred yards away.

"Do you think this is far enough that he can't hear us?" I said.

"From all my studies, yes," my mother said. "It looks dark in there.
I don't think he's home."

"What about a manservant?" Rose said. "In the movies vampires
always have manservants."

"I didn't see one when I was here before," I said.

"You were here before?" Mama snapped.

I dismissed her concern with a wave. "Yes, and I'm still alive. At
least I have an idea of where to go. So. How do we get in?"

My mother pulled a hairpin from her hair. "Leave that to me."

Ten minutes later the three of us were stumbling around in the
dark manor.

Someone clomped on my toe. "Ow!"

"Sorry," Rose whimpered. "Glinda, we need light."

A moment later a ball of water glowing with light appeared in my
mother's palm.

"Show-off," I murmured.

She shot me a dark look. "Sorry," I said. "Forgot about the truce."

"Open your hand," she commanded.

Two more balls of light appeared—one in my palm and one in Rose's.

"We need to split up," I said.

"Oh no," Rose argued. "That's how people die in the movies."

"What is it with you comparing everything to movies?" I said.

She shrugged. "I just thought popular culture was an easy reference to make."

"You have the pig with you."

"I'll stay with Rose," Mama said, sighing. "We'll check down here."

"I'll head to the bedroom," I said. "If there's proof the vamp did something to Jimmy, then I want to know about it."

I slowly stepped up the marble staircase. See? Manor. This house stuck out like a sore thumb on steroids.

The ball of water and light wobbled in my hand. I was surprised my mother hadn't been really cocky and stuck a goldfish in the middle of it.

Her voiced floated up the staircase. "I didn't put a fish in it because the light might've hurt its eyes."

I shook my head. Typical that she'd figure out what I was thinking.

I sighed and pushed on, remembering I was in the lair of a vampire. If he caught us, we'd be supper—literally. We had to be quick and quiet.

At the top of the stairs several doors broke off to the left. I slowly opened the first one and found it to be a guest bedroom.

The second door was the same, as was the third. Finally I reached a set of double doors. The hinges squeaked when I opened them. I cringed. Thank goodness the vamp wasn't here.

Behind the door sat a suite of rooms. The furnishings were simple if not lavishly built.

"Bingo," I whispered.

The first thing I noticed was the smell. The room smelled of Thorne—wet grass, vanilla and a hint of musk.

Not that I'd wanted to notice how the man smelled, but I couldn't help it when he stood right over me the night that Langdon had been killed.

Lots of dark wood sprinkled the room. From what I could tell the walls were a hunter green. Yes, I walked right up to them with the ball.

A glass case full of mementoes stood in one corner. Relics from the past had been placed carefully on each shelf—an old pair of eyeglasses, an antique apothecary bottle, a WWII helmet, and a marble statue of a goddess that looked like it had been plucked right out of Ancient Rome.

Perhaps these were memories from his past. If so, Thorne was old —I mean really old. So old I didn't want to think about it.

I moved on, going over to his wardrobe. There wasn't a closet in the room. Instead Thorne used an old wooden wardrobe to store his clothes. I opened it and found the usual—shirts, slacks, socks—nothing interesting.

I frowned and faced the space. The walls were lined with personal pictures—some taken with a camera, some painted.

Like I said, the guy was old.

That seemed to be the most incriminating thing about him. There wasn't anything in the space that suggested he had anything to do with Jimmy's disappearance.

I crossed to his mirror, where a small stool sat in front of it. I stared at my own reflection. In the low light, holding the orb, I looked to have deep shadows under my eyes.

I needed to get some sleep.

But I wouldn't sleep well until I found Jimmy and ensured the stability of my company.

Something draped over the stool caught my attention. I moved the watery ball of light to it.

The plaid pattern suggested a shirt. I picked it up. It *was* a shirt. As I held the orb behind it, I realized that not only was it a shirt, but it was also a clue.

I gasped.

The back had been shredded exactly like Jimmy's.

I knew it! I knew the bloodsucker had something to do with Jimmy's disappearance. He'd probably done it! Why the heck would a town of witches trust a gang of vampires to do their justice for them?

It was so totally wrong.

Vampires were ruthless killers—everyone knew that. They drank blood—human blood. A town full of witches was a perfect feeding ground for them. Why couldn't anyone see that?

I balled the shirt and tucked it in my waistband. "Let's see what the mayor says when I show her this."

I rushed downstairs and found my mother and Rose in the kitchen. The refrigerator door was open, and Rose stood in front of it.

"I wonder if he has an apple," she said.

My mother peered over her shoulder. "There's one. In the back. I'm sure he won't notice if it's missing."

Rose plucked it from the refrigerator. "Good eye, Glinda."

"What are y'all doing?" I hissed.

Rose shrugged. The refrigerator door stood wide open, illuminating both my mother and aunt. "I'm getting a snack for Pig. She's hungry."

Rose handed the apple to Pig, and the little potbellied swine sniffed it before delicately taking it in her jaws.

I slapped my forehead. "You're supposed to be looking for clues."

"There might be a clue in the fridge," my mother pointed out.

I folded my arms. "Like what?"

"Bags of blood."

I prayed to Jesus for serenity but received none. "Are there bags of blood inside?"

"Well no," Rose admitted.

Then it occurred to me that it was strange that a vampire would have a refrigerator, much less food.

I crossed to them. "Let me see in there."

Rose moved out of the way, and I sneaked a peek. It was a fully stocked fridge with lots of vegetables—asparagus, zucchini, yellow squash, artichokes, and also meat wrapped in butcher paper.

"Is this guy just pretending to be a vampire?" I mused.

"Oh, I don't think so, Charming," Rose said. "The way he looked at me sent a swirl right to my woman parts. Only a vampire can do that after you've gone through menopause."

"Thank you, Aunt Rose." I shook my head. "I really appreciate too much information when we're sneaking around a house," I added with a dose of sarcasm.

"We haven't found any clues," Rose said. "Have you?"

"Yes!" I pulled the shirt from my waistband. "It's ripped. Exactly like we found in the house."

"Let me see that." My mother plucked it from my hand. "How strange. It looks like whoever did this didn't draw any blood."

"I know. That vampire must be quite talented with his claws."

Mama shook her head. "I don't think this is the work of a vampire."

I frowned. "You don't?"

"Let me see if we can figure out who it belonged to."

My eyelids flared with surprise. "Can you do that with magic?"

"I could," she said smugly, "but luckily it's stitched right here in the collar."

Now why hadn't I looked there? "What's it say?"

She turned her palm, and the ball of light slipped from her hand and buoyed beside her, illuminating the shirt.

I leaned in and gasped. "Langdon Huggins. Oh my gosh. That's the man who was murdered—or spelled or something. He had a ripped shirt? But why would Thorne rip his shirt and leave him alive only to return later and kill him?"

"That's what I'm saying," Mama said, "I don't think—"

From the front of the house a lock snicked. I shot Rose and Mama a frantic look.

"He's back. Quick! We've got to get out of here." I glanced around and spied a door. "Through there!"

Rose closed the refrigerator. I picked up Pig, who dropped what was left of her apple and immediately started squealing. I capped a hand over her mouth, but that only muffled her sound. It didn't drown it out.

"Hurry!"

We rushed to the door just as I heard the front one open. A light snapped on in the foyer.

My mother, ever the thinker, silently unlocked the back door with magic. It opened and the three of us dashed out. Pig leaped from my arms and headed back inside the house.

The three of us stood frozen.

"We can't go after her," I said.

"Why'd she go back in?" Mama said.

Rose gave me a dark look. "Because of someone who shall remain nameless, Pig dropped her apple."

We rushed into a line of hedges and waited. It only took about ten seconds before we could hear Thorne yelling at Pig.

"Get out of here! What're you doing? Why is my back door open?"

"We're dead meat," I whispered. "He's going to drain us dry."

At that point Thorne had flipped a switch in the kitchen. I watched him chase Pig. The potbellied swine was no competition for the vampire with cheetah-like speed.

He snatched her up and walked to the back door. Thorne gently placed her on the ground, shut the door and went back in.

He didn't say one word, but there was no doubt he knew he'd been broken into.

"Let's get out of here," I said.

Mama nodded. "Now that I can see Pig, I'll transport us."

I held onto the hedge and closed my eyes. Transportation by magic was never fun. Air *swooshed* beside my ears. My stomach fell as if I were riding a roller coaster.

Another *swoosh* and I felt a flat surface beneath me. Light pricked my closed lids, and I hesitated before opening them.

Mama spoke. "You can open them, Charming. We're back at the house."

She knew I hated magical travel. I blinked my eyes open. I sat on the kitchen floor while Mama and Rose perched in chairs at the table.

My mother shot a disgusted look at the lime-green table. "We really need to talk this house into updating. I think I'd prefer stainless or even black slate appliances and quartz countertops."

I stretched my stiff legs. Pig lay on the floor, scratching her back on the tile.

"Do you think he knew it was us?" I said.

"He'll figure it out if he sees your car," Mama said.

"Crap."

She smiled. "Don't worry. I camouflaged it. It now looks like a brand-new shrub was planted. The vampire will never notice."

"Thank goodness." I sighed with relief. "That was close."

"Too close," Rose said. "We're lucky we got out of that alive. I'm surprised he didn't keep Pig."

I grimaced. "I'm sorry I almost got y'all caught. Got us all thrown in jail, or whatever they have in this town."

"It's called mother-daughter bonding." Mama winked at me. "Everyone's safe. We're fine."

"Did you get the shirt?"

My mother placed a hand on her chest mockingly. "What kind of mother would I be if I didn't make sure to take the evidence?"

I grinned. "Let's see it."

She unfurled the ripped shirt and laid it on the table. We circled it, inspecting the specimen. "There's no blood. It's like I said, Charming, I don't think the vampire did it."

"Then why would he have it? Langdon wasn't wearing this when he was murdered. Why would the vampire have the murder victim's shirt?"

"He *is* the police," Rose commented.

I shook my head. "Y'all know vampires can't be the police of witches."

"This one is," Mama said in a clipped voice. "But I don't think these are claw marks from a vampire."

"You said that before," I said. "What are they if not that?"

She stared at the shirt and pushed the fabric apart. "This didn't come from the outside."

I hiked a skeptical brow. "Meaning?"

"She doesn't think Langdon was attacked," Rose interpreted.

"Then what happened if he wasn't attacked?"

My mother pinned her lips together in thought. She studied the shirt for another moment before taking a step back and looking over it as if she were perusing a priceless work of art.

"This man wasn't attacked. Whatever happened to him came from him. He tore through the shirt himself."

"What?" I said in disbelief.

"Langdon changed into something big and powerful enough that he ripped through the shirt." Her gaze flickered to me. Sorrow filled her eyes. "I'm sorry to say that whatever changed Langdon also changed your friend, Jimmy."

I frowned. "I don't understand."

"Charming," she said slowly, "this looks like a powerful metamorphosis spell. If Langdon was killed because of it, Jimmy may already be dead as well."

FOURTEEN

The next day my mother magically got my car back from where it had been parked near Thorne's house. I told Mama and Aunt Rose that I was going to Air Town to work on some matches, but I was really going for another purpose.

"Charming," Mama said before I walked out the door.

"Yes?"

"Where did you get that hideous broom? It looks like something the cat coughed up."

"Oh, I got it in Air Town. Belinda gave it to me. Watch out, it spanks."

Her brows shot up. "Oh? And did you get Pig in Earth Town?"

"Yep, another gift."

"Do me a favor and stop taking gifts from witches."

"Why?"

She bristled. "Because the next gift from Fire Town will probably be a life-size dragon. The last thing we need is for the house to burn down."

I rolled my eyes. "Sure thing."

I left and headed over to Air Town. Something nudged at the back of my mind—why would my mother be concerned with me receiving gifts from witches?

Maybe it had something to do with that silly prophecy. I blew a strand of hair from my face. Yeah, right.

I parked on the outskirts of Air Town and exited the car. I'd finally had enough sense to stop walking around town in heels and had opted for stylish sneakers, capri jeans and a pink gingham shirt.

I might not be in the city, but I'd be darned if I wasn't going to look cute. The only thing I lacked was a magnolia blossom to tuck behind my ear.

Speaking of, the magnolia trees were in full bloom. There were even a few cowcumber trees with beautiful full blossoms similar to magnolias.

I found Belinda doing goat yoga with a bunch of other witches, and yes, they each had their goats and were performing the moves.

She saw me and broke away from the group. "Charming, are you here to see me?"

"Sort of. The first thing I wanted to talk to you about was Cap."

Hesitation filled her eyes. "I'm sorry?"

"Look, I know the two of y'all used to date. I know you broke up, but I believe y'all are supposed to be together."

She shook her head. "It's against the law."

Crap. This whole illegal intermingling thing really had a hold on the town. I had to find a way to prove my theory that keeping people apart was what was killing the town. But how?

"Okay, well, since you won't be convinced so easily, can you point me to where Langdon Huggins lived?"

Belinda gave me directions, and I headed off toward Langdon's. I didn't exactly know what I was doing, but I figured I should just fake it until I made it.

I reached the house and knocked on the door. A tall man about thirty with sun streaked and windblown blond hair and wearing Bermuda shorts with no shirt answered.

"Can I help you?" he said in a surfer-type voice. I nearly rolled my eyes.

Only in Air Town.

"Yes sir, my name is Charming Calhoun. I'm with Southern Belles and Spells Matchmakers, and I wanted to speak to you about Langdon."

"He was my brother." The man cocked his brow in suspicion. "Dudette, did you send that dude here? The one who was trying to match Langdon to that Belinda girl?"

"Yes. Do you have a few minutes to talk?"

He surveyed the landscape behind me and moved aside. "Come in. Watch the mess. I live on pizza."

I followed him in. The room was full of all the things air wizards would use—wind chimes, a glass container with a large mouth for trapping wind and even hanging sticks that looked like a type of archaic mobile. I was surprised I didn't see a surfboard.

"My name's Jamison."

"Nice to meet you."

He settled into a chair and motioned for me to do the same. I picked over a few empty pizza boxes and sat on the edge of a chair with a brown stain in the rear.

"What can I do for you, Miss Calhoun?"

"I know that my company matched your brother to Belinda."

Jamison laughed. "Even I could see that match was wrong. Way wrong. Belinda would never go for the likes of my brother—he drank too much, swore too much. Dude, he was not into the pure life." Jamison rapped his knuckles on the chair arm. "Let's just say it wasn't a good match."

"So I've learned. Your brother didn't appear to be your typical air wizard. He was in Earth Town the night he was murdered."

Jamison's mouth set in a grim line. "He went to confront Cap about Belinda. Thought Cap was the reason that Langdon and Belinda weren't working. That they still had something going on."

I clicked my tongue. "But it wasn't true."

Jamison raked his fingers through his stiff hair. "No, not true at all."

"Did you notice anything strange about your brother leading up to his murder?"

His eyes narrowed to steely bolts of lightning. "What do you mean?"

I shrugged, trying to look as innocent as possible. "Oh, I don't know…him ripping through his clothes, that sort of thing?"

Jamison laughed. It was loud and throaty, welcoming. For the first time I noticed his eyes danced with light.

"Dudette, I didn't notice anything like that, but before your matchmaker guy came along, Langdon was hanging out at night a lot." He paused and scrubbed a palm down his cheek. "I shouldn't be telling you this—a stranger."

Oh, now I really wanted to know the dirty details. "What is it? Mr. Huggins, I'm trying to help. Where was he hanging out?"

"He told me," Jamison said quietly. "But I found it hard to believe."

"Where did he say? Please."

He pursed his lips a moment before answering. "My bro was hanging out at the tavern."

My jaw dropped. "With the vampires?"

Jamison nodded. "Yep. With the vampires."

I THANKED Jamison and handed him my card before leaving. "Do you mind doing me a favor?"

"What's that?"

"Do you have a girlfriend or significant other?"

He rubbed the back of his neck shyly. "No, ma'am, I sure don't."

"Then would you mind if I matched you?"

He glanced around nervously. "Will it hurt?"

I laughed. "No, it doesn't hurt."

"Then no, I guess I don't mind."

I pulled a slip of paper from my folder and held it in front of him. "Place your hand on top."

He squinted at me. "It's not, like, gonna reach out and bite me, is it?"

"It won't. Trust me."

He cocked a brow. "Just touch it?"

I nodded cheerfully. "That's all you have to do."

Jamison obeyed, and a moment later words flared on the page. I saw the name on the bottom and the description that she was an air witch.

Then I brushed my hand over Jamison's under the guise that I was taking the paper from him.

A completely different witch appeared in my head. She had fiery red hair and wore clothing that resembled flames.

"A fire witch," I murmured.

"What's that?" he said.

I whisked the paper away. "Mr. Huggins, I will be in touch with you. I know who your soul mate is; I just have to find her."

Before he could ask another question, I left with more proof that the magical inbreeding in Witch's Forge needed to stop.

I arrived at the tavern a few minutes later. Since it was daytime, I figured it was acceptable for me to enter.

The same bartender from the other night rubbed down glasses.

"You're not looking for trouble, are you?" he said.

"Why? Are you offering it in a glass? Perhaps a shot of trouble to start my day?"

He extended his hand with a laugh. "Name's Kirk Glisson."

"How do you do? Charming Calhoun."

"Can I get you something?"

"No, but I have some questions for you, if you have time to answer."

He winked at me. Was he flirting? I didn't go for bald men, which Kirk was, but I was certain I could match him with a lady who did.

He leaned both arms on the table. "What've you got?"

"I heard that Langdon Huggins was hanging out here some. Is that true?"

Kirk narrowed his eyes. "That's not the sort of question I expected."

I winked. "I like to surprise people. It's a thing with me."

Kirk filled a glass with water and slid it over to me. "So you want to know about Langdon."

"Yes. Tell me everything," I joked, *not joked*.

"As a matter of fact he was around one night. Met some fire witches."

That was a surprise. "Fire witches?"

He nodded. "Outside. That's what I saw. He didn't come in. No one does—except you."

The door opened and wouldn't you know it, but Thorne the Evil Vampire stood in the frame, his eyes blazing.

"I've been looking for you," he directed at me.

I leaned against the bar and batted my lashes at him. "Now you've found me. I was just here talking to Kirk. Because, you know, *it's daytime* and I can be in the bar and not be run off by a bunch of blood-sucking vampires."

He stormed over to me, his eyes shooting flames. "We need to talk," he seethed.

So I guess he somehow figured out that I had broken into his house. Rose probably ran and told him. Wouldn't that just be my luck?

"Oh? What would you like to talk about?"

"In my office." He motioned for me to walk to the back of the bar.

I didn't bother hiding my confusion. "Your office?"

Annoyance filled his voice. "It's in the back."

"Of the bar?"

He ground his teeth. "Follow me."

I followed him to the back and then down a flight of stairs. Thorne opened a steel door, revealing a cavernous space. Red clay walls, burning gas lamps and iron bars all filled the space.

"What is this?" I said, full of wonder. "Your vampire torture room?"

"It's the jail." He shook his head, perturbed. "And my office."

"You have an office down here?" I didn't bother keeping the surprise from my voice.

"Yes." He stopped at an iron gate and unlocked it. Anger flashed in his silver eyes. "And a jail, which we often lock people up in. So that's why it's best not to be seen at the tavern at night."

I crossed my arms. "Not because a bunch of big bad vampires hang out there?"

"No. Because for one, your reputation might be at risk and two, because the men are always looking for action at night. You don't want to give a gang of vampires—"

"Reason to attack?" I finished for him.

He scowled and opened the door. "Exactly." Thorne gestured for me to walk through. I did and waited for him.

"But I thought you said they don't feed on witches."

"They don't," he growled. "My office is here."

Thorne opened another door. A desk, a couple of chairs and lots of knickknacks—like at his house—sprinkled the shelves.

He sat behind the dark oak desk and gestured for me to sit. I felt like I'd been called into the principal's office.

I obliged, crossing my legs and staring at him. No way was I going to give the bloodsucker any idea that he had an advantage over me.

Thorne studied me. I could feel the iciness of his gaze, like pinpricks dancing across my flesh.

"Did you have fun breaking into my house last night?"

"I have no idea what you're talking about."

He drummed his fingers on the desk. Thorne's lips coiled into a smirk. "That pig is very cute. Is she yours?"

"I don't have a pig."

"Do you want to return what you took from me?"

I hiked a shoulder and met his stare. "I don't know what you're talking about. I didn't take anything. I didn't break into your house."

He relaxed into the leather chair. "Aside from the fact that the whole house smelled like you—"

I reared back. "What do I smell like? And I think it's really creepy that you go around sniffing people."

"First of all," he said sharply, "I am cursed with a sense of smell that most men would beg for."

"I doubt it."

"Secondly, I don't go around sniffing people, but most have a particular scent, you included."

I winked at him. "You didn't answer what that scent is."

Thorne flexed his fingers. "You smell like fresh dew and lemongrass."

"Sexy," I said sarcastically.

His jaw flexed. "For your information a natural scent that mimics natural things is better than a fake scent sprayed on that tries to smell like nature. The fake always sours."

His gaze snagged on mine, and I felt my heartbeat flutter in my throat.

"So you're complimenting me, how nice. Must make you feel good that you can tell the lowly witches that they aren't just food, they're individual meals."

He slammed a hand on the desk. "I don't eat witches in this town."

"Oh, but you do in other towns?"

"Stop twisting my words."

"Then stop speaking," I yelled.

We silently scowled at each other, both our gazes pinned to the other.

Thorne spoke first. "I found this in my house." He plucked something from his pocket and slid it across the table. "Even if I hadn't recognized your scent, this betrayed you."

I peered at what he'd presented—my business card. Dang! It must've slipped from my pocket. How stupid I'd been. If I was going to break into people's houses, I really needed to be better about not leaving evidence behind.

My cheeks burned. There was no getting out of this. But maybe there was. "I must've given it to you when we first met."

He shook his head. "No. You never gave it to me. I, unlike the rest of this town, don't require your services. I don't need a matchmaker, thank you very much."

"Why? Did you accidentally kill your last wife? Drink her blood?"

"Stop it! Your anger toward me isn't going to stop me from

throwing you in a cell. You broke the law. I have proof you were in my house, and I'm missing something."

I should've been afraid. I should've been scared for my life. I was alone with a vampire. The last time that had happened hadn't worked out so well—I'd lived...barely.

But instead of being afraid, I was angry. This vampire had duped the entire town into thinking he was a good guy. Even though my mother said the shirt had been spelled, Thorne had still kept it, and I was convinced he was keeping things from me about Jimmy.

"I have the shirt," I admitted.

His shoulders relaxed. "Now. Was that so hard?"

"What's going on?"

"I can't tell you."

I fisted my hands. "My friend is missing."

"I'm in the middle of an investigation."

"One man is dead. Jimmy might already be dead. What are you doing about it? Sitting in here interrogating me, the one person we both know had nothing to do with it, when you should be out combing the streets."

He raked his fingers through the thick waves of his hair. A blond tendril slipped from his dark locks and fell into his eyes. "I don't need you to tell me how to do my job."

"You need somebody."

He smirked but said nothing.

Curiosity got the better of me. "What is it?"

"I'm debating whether I want to throw you in a cell or ask you over for dinner."

A sucker punch to the gut. I didn't expect that. Worse, my cheeks burned under his steely stare. I finally ground out, "I will never have dinner with you."

He grinned. "Which is fine by me because I don't have dinner with witches."

"I despise vampires."

"Really?" He hiked a perfectly arched brow. "I never would've guessed. I'm not too fond of witches, myself."

DEADLY SPELLS AND A SOUTHERN BELLE

I threw my hands in the air. "Then what are you doing here? Why would you live in a town full of witches and you don't like them? How do I even know you're looking for Jimmy? You don't like witches, so why would you help us?"

He rose abruptly. "You don't like vampires. I'm going to guess one almost killed you."

I froze and stared at him. I could feel anger pouring out of me and shooting straight to him. "That," I said coldly, "is none of your business."

His jaw clenched. "I'll show you the door. But I want Langdon's shirt back."

"I don't have it," I said smartly.

"Where is it?"

Would it incriminate me more to tell him? How much bigger of a hole could I really dig for myself?

When I didn't answer, he said, "I'll stop by the courthouse and get it myself."

"How do you know where I'm staying?"

Before showing me from his office, Thorne said, "Everyone knows where you're staying. It's not a secret."

With that, he locked the gate leading to the jail behind me and walked away.

FIFTEEN

$\mathcal{I}$ had to get home to warn my mother about Thorne. He'd want that shirt and he'd want it soon. I was headed back when someone calling my name caught my attention.

"Yoo-hoo, Charming! Hey, girl! What're you doing?"

Kimberly bobbed up to me, her red lips so puffed up they looked to overtake her face.

"You feeling okay? Had an allergic reaction?"

She shook her head. "No, I thought I'd try a new spell where I make my lips bigger—you know, to get ready to meet my soul mate and all—but it backfired like every spell does in this town. I don't even know why I tried it, but I thought it was sure-fire."

"Kimberly, tell me something."

"Yes?" She raised a Coke and slurped through the straw. "What is it?"

"What happens to your magic if you leave town? Does it get better?"

Kimberly shook her head. "No, you can leave, but the curse of the town stays with you. Apparently in its heyday Witch's Forge was booming. Witches and vampires mingled, even regular folks would come—hence all the shops to attract them. They didn't know about the magic, of course, people were very careful not to reveal too much but this town was full of power. It was supposedly beautiful. I know the mayor thinks getting people married will help change it back. Maybe it will. I don't know. At the very least it'll boost morale."

I smirked. "Yeah, I guess so. I've questioned Mayor Dixon's expectations."

Kimberly laughed. "Girl, I don't think anyone has expectations. We just want a distraction."

Just then Thorne stormed from the tavern. He took one look at me and shook his head.

When he was out of earshot, Kimberly released a deep breath. "Oh, wouldn't you love to let him sink his fangs into you?"

I shrank back, appalled. "Absolutely not. A vampire and a witch? That's disgusting."

She hiked a shoulder. "Thorne's not. He's dreamy. But he hates it here, being trapped and all."

Trapped? Now this was news. "What do you mean?"

"Haven't you heard?" She sidled in closer and glanced right and left to make sure no one could overhear. "Apparently Thorne did something bad, very bad. Made his father angry and was banished here. His dad is some big froo-froo vampire. He found out we needed a police guy and got Thorne the job, but Thorne can't leave. That's why he's so bitter and unsocial."

"What about his band of merry men? What's their excuse for being so horrible?"

Kimberly snorted. "Band of merry men! That's hilarious. Oh, they're just vampires who work with him. They leave whenever they want. Not Thorne. He's stuck here. There's some sort of vampire magic that keeps him in the area."

"So *that* magic works?"

"Mmm hmmm. I don't know how long his sentence is, but it's for a long time."

I raised my hand to stop her. "So you're saying a criminal is the chief of police?"

"Not a criminal. He just ticked off his dad. But don't ask me how or why. I've told you all I know." Kimberly pressed a finger to her lips. "That's just between us, okay?"

"My lips are sealed."

Kimberly brushed her fingers over her mouth. "Speaking of lips. I need to figure out a way to fix these. I know a water witch who's good with that sort of thing."

I fluffed my hair. "If your friend can't help, find me; my mom can probably do something."

Her eyes flared with excitement. "Oh, are you serious? To have Glinda Calhoun work magic on me would be striking a line through a goal on my bucket list."

Was she kidding? Really the celebrity surrounding my mother was so annoying.

I smile tightly. "Sure. I'll make it happen. Just let me know."

"And I'll be on the lookout for my soul mate. He'll be arriving by train, you say? It's taking everything I've got not to sit at the station every day."

"Um, let's not resort to that," I said pointedly.

"Don't worry." She swatted away my concern playfully. "I'm not going to camp out there or anything."

Right. "Well, I'll see you soon."

"See ya."

I walked back to the courthouse and found my mother and aunt had created a room devoted completely to magic. Potions and powders lined the shelves. A large tome of spells lay open on a lectern.

"I don't think that's the spell that was used in this case," Mama said.

Rose peered at the book. "It looks to me like a jumping bean spell. Like that Langdon fellow was inside his shirt one minute and jumped out the next. Don't you think so, Pig?"

From a corner, Pig snorted as if she could understand human.

"I'm not the most talented witch," I said.

I could practically see my mother biting her tongue to make sure she didn't respond smartly.

"However," I continued, "I will have to say that in this case I think my mother is right. There's no way a jumping bean spell was used."

"Thank you, Charming," Mama said. "Whatever has you flushed?"

My hand flashed to my neck. "I'm not flushed."

"You most certainly are. Your neck is pink and your cheeks are splotched."

I was not flushed. I didn't know what she was talking about.

"Anyway." I poked the air. "We have a problem. Thorne knows we broke into his house."

"Who's Thorne?" Rose said.

I rolled my eyes. "The evil vampire who has the hots for you."

"Oh, him? Well, if Thorne wants the shirt, I suppose he should have it."

"He's the police around here. He has to have it." I gave my mom a reproachful look. "So whatever experiment you're doing, you'll have to stop."

"Rose, hand me those scissors." Rose handed a pair of silver shears to Mama. My mother proceeded to snip a slice of the shirt from the back. "What he won't know won't hurt him." She shrugged. "Besides, we have to keep some of it so I can figure out what sort of spell it is. It will also help us pair it to Jimmy's ripped shirt—make sure it's the same spell on both. Not that the shirt will help too much, since everyone's powers in this town are topsy-turvy except for ours. The spell may look like one thing but really be another."

"Witch's Forge is a unique place," I murmured.

"So it is." She raised the snippet of cloth and balled up the rest of the shirt. The doorbell rang. "Looks like the vampire is right on time. I want to see up close this creature that has you all flushed, Charming. There must be something very alluring about him."

"There's nothing alluring about a vampire," I argued.

"Oh, that's not true," Rose said. "Vampires can be very alluring. That's often how they catch their prey—by seducing them. The next thing you know, you don't have any blood left."

"Thank you, Aunt Rose." I darted in front of my mother, blocking her path. "You don't have to give him the shirt. I'll do it."

"Nonsense," she said in her tone of superiority, "I want to meet him."

With a flicker of her hand, my mother evaporated and appeared at the door, her fingers on the knob. She shot me a smug look and opened it.

Thorne stood on the other side. His expression was sort of a simmering glower, the kind of anger that didn't look to dissipate anytime soon.

At least not when the situation concerned me.

"I take it you're the vampire," Mama said.

"My reputation precedes me."

She offered her hand, and he took it. "I'm Glinda Calhoun. I believe you know my daughter, Charming. This is my aunt, Rose."

"I'm Thorne Blackwood." He ignored me and focused on Rose. "I have met Ms. Rose."

Rose winked at him. I wanted to die. "It's wonderful to see you."

All I wanted was for my mother to hand over the shirt so Thorne could leave, but that isn't what happened.

"I understand the three of us may have misbehaved and took something important from you."

Thorne didn't say anything.

"Mr. Blackwood, I would like to help. I'm not sure if you're aware of my talents, but I can assure you I am a powerful witch. I'd like to assist you in figuring out what sort of spell caused this problem. I've already been pouring over my books." She paused to look him up and down, giving Thorne the same contemplative look I was used to being on the receiving end of. "That is assuming you've realized a spell is the cause of the shredded shirt."

His harsh expression melted, and his lips slowly curved. "I have realized it must be magical."

"Good. That's settled. We will help you figure out what could've caused this. Now, would you like to stay for dinner? I'm afraid I can't offer any fresh meat or blood; we were going to have fried chicken."

My eyelids flared, and I shot my mother a look that clearly suggested she was supposed to stop, right then, and not ask him to join us. Why would she do that? Ask the evil vampire to break bread or bones with us?

My mother ignored my pained expression and smiled at Thorne. "Well, would you like to join us?"

Thorne's gaze darted to me. I shot him an annoyed look. The corners of his mouth turned up even more. This amused him! Oh, great.

"Yes," he finally answered, "I'd love to."

I quickly intervened. "I'm sure you have things to do, right? Like find Jimmy and all that? I mean, perhaps this isn't a good time."

Thorne patted his flat belly. "No, this is a fine time. I could use a break."

"Cave jail getting to be too much for you?"

He ignored my jab. "Can I help set the table?"

Rose beamed. "You and Charming can set the table while Glinda and I finish the meal."

"We don't even have a dining room," I fumed.

"That's ridiculous, Charming," Mama said. "All you have to do is ask for it. Everyone knows that."

My mother strode past me, clapping her hands. "House, we need a dining room and a table that will seat at least six. Wall sconces would be nice, too—oh, and a buffet filled with china."

"Would you also like the house to polish the silver?"

"Good point," she said. "You heard what Charming said. Polished silver."

I shook my head. *Why me?* A moment later, after the house coughed and rumbled, a dining room sprouted off the front hallway.

I shot Thorne a dark look. "Well, what are you waiting for? Help me set the table."

Without one iota of an argument, Thorne silently followed. I opened the buffet's drawers and found everything we needed, handing off the silverware to Thorne.

"If it bothers you that I'm staying, I can leave," he said quietly.

"Why would it bother me? You could just attack any of us and drink our blood for your meal, at any moment. Why should I be bothered by that?"

"Charming!" My mother appeared in the doorway. "I didn't raise you to be rude to guests. Now apologize to Mr. Blackwood."

I mean, was it really necessary to be treated like a five-year-old?

"Apologize," she repeated.

I needed to get my mom to leave this town ASAP. She was cramping my style.

But I plastered on my sweetest smile and tipped my head down like a submissive lady. "I'm sorry, Mr. Blackwood, for suggesting you might want to snack on one of us instead of fried chicken." I turned to Mama. "Was that better?"

"No."

"It's okay, Ms. Calhoun," Thorne directed to my mother. "You should've been here when I arrived to take the police chief job. Those who didn't fear me still hated me. I'm used to it."

"It won't be that way in this house," she said, giving me a look so stern it could've melted my hair.

I withered. "Sorry," I muttered to Thorne. I sort-of meant it.

I shut my mouth and finished setting plates. I moved past Thorne, being sure to keep a wide berth lest he smell the blood pulsing at my throat and want to take a nibble.

I'd laid all the plates, glasses and coffee cups except for the last. I leaned over to set it at the same time that Thorne crossed over to place the last spoon.

We were both going for the same side. My hand brushed his arm, knocking the cup from its saucer.

Quick as mercury, Thorne's hand flashed in the air. He caught the cup and extended it toward me as if it were some sort of peace offering.

"For you," he said softly.

I dragged my gaze from his hand, where for the first time I noticed Thorne wore a fitted black suit jacket with a white shirt underneath. His silver eyes softened as our gazes met. I peered at him as if hoping some sort of secret about the man would be revealed.

Pain flashed in his eyes, and Thorne quickly looked away.

"Thank you," I mumbled.

"You're welcome."

Tension filled the room as if the sudden dissolving of our dammed-up anger for each other had caused a shift that neither of us knew how to deal with.

If we weren't annoyed with one another, what could we be?

Mama sailed in. "Dinner's ready!" She carried a tray piled high with steaming fried chicken. It smelled like heaven had swooped down to earth. "Rose is bringing the mashed potatoes."

Rose entered, Pig tucked under one arm and mashed potatoes in the other.

Thorne quickly took the potatoes from her and settled them on the table.

Rose surveyed the place settings before cocking her head in confusion. "Where's Pig's spot?"

"On the floor," Mama chirped.

Rose obeyed and we settled into our seats. As Mama passed the food, she fixed an eye on Thorne.

"Now, Mr. Blackwood," she said.

"Yes?"

She threaded her fingers and steepled them under her chin. "Tell us everything about you. All your deep, dark secrets. Because I know you have them."

SIXTEEN

horne cleared his throat. Was the vampire nervous? Did they get nervous? I doubted it. But there he sat, clearing his gizzard like he had a gigantic frog stuck in it.

"You want to know my secrets?"

"Yes," Mama said with a hint of smugness. "I know you have at least one, and I want to hear it. It makes no sense to me that a vampire would be policing a town full of witches—even a cursed town, or whatever is screwing with this place. So. I have to assume that you did something or ticked someone off to be forced here. After all, a person like you would want more in life than being stuck here, high in the Smokies where the Bigfoots roam."

Bigfoot? I mouthed to her. With a flick of her hand Mama dismissed my question.

Thorne chuckled. "What makes you think I want more than to live in Witch's Forge?"

"Please. Don't play me for a fool. I'm helping you, remember? After dinner we'll discuss what I've found so far."

"But we haven't discovered anything," Rose blurted.

Mother kicked her under the table. "Ow," Rose said.

116

Thorne swiped a napkin over his face to hide a smile. "I'll tell you what I can. How's that?"

"Perfect. Maybe then Charming will be convinced you're not a bad vampire after all."

"I never said he was a bad vampire," I protested.

"You act like it," Thorne said. "Your hate for me is scorching."

I couldn't argue. "You haven't exactly been welcoming either."

"You broke into my house!"

"For a greater cause. To find my friend."

His exasperation nearly blew the ceiling off the room. "I'm looking for him."

"You also have a death to solve."

"They're connected," he fumed.

"Now you agree with me."

"I never said I didn't." Thorne glared at me and then turned back to my mother, because apparently dealing with her was easier.

Haha. Joke was on him. Mama was ten times worse than me.

"You're right." He slid a knife into the fried chicken. Sheesh, this guy was so well-mannered he made me look like a hick when I picked up my drumstick and sank my teeth into it.

I watched closely to see if he'd actually eat any of the cooked flesh.

Thorne paused with his fork near his mouth. "My father and I got into an argument."

"What sort of argument?" my mother asked.

"The sort that involved me being sent here."

"So you were banished."

"More like imprisoned," he said. "I can't leave."

"At all?" Rose asked, astonished.

Thorne shook his head. The fork still hovered in front of his lips. "No."

"I hope you don't mind me prying," Mama said, "but what could you have done that chained you here?"

Sorrow filled his eyes. "I saved a woman from death."

Mama shot me a look that said, *You see? He's not that bad.* My return expression said, *I'm still not buying it.*

"You saved her?" Mama repeated.

Thorne nodded. "The thing is, she wasn't supposed to be saved. She was dying, so I turned her."

"Into a vampire?" I said coldly.

His gaze flickered to me. "Yes."

"And for that your father banished you?" Rose said. "Well, I think what you did was wonderful."

"Give him a medal," I said.

"Charming," my mother warned.

I hiked a shoulder in innocence. "What?"

"Do not let your personal prejudice infiltrate our dinner." She glanced to Thorne. "You have to forgive my daughter; she has a bad history with vampires."

"As do you," I shot back.

"Some of us can forgive," she replied coldly.

Thorne nodded. A slash of dark hair fell into his eyes. "I understand. Most witches despise us."

"Well, Charming isn't much of a witch," Mama added.

I wanted to die from embarrassment.

"Oh, I don't know," Thorne said. "She managed to sneak into my house while I wasn't there. Seems like it would take some magic to do that."

"It's not like you have hellhounds guarding the place," I said.

"He's at the vet," Thorne said smartly.

Well, touché.

"So tell us," Mama continued. Because my mother couldn't leave the conversation there, where the vampire turned someone into another vamp, probably against her will. Instead she had to pry more. "Did you love this woman? The one who wasn't supposed to be turned?"

"Yes—no," he quickly added. "Not the way you think. I wasn't in love with her."

"Then why did you turn her?" I said sarcastically, fully expecting him to reveal some selfish answer.

"Because my father loved her," Thorne answered.

How I hated him.

"So romantic," Rose mused. "You didn't love her but because your father did, you made her immortal."

"Please," I muttered.

"Why didn't your father want her saved?" Mama asked.

Thorne settled his fork on the table. It still had the chicken on it, I noted.

"My father isn't my biological father," he explained. "He's the man who turned me. Several years ago my father made a law that no one could be turned without permission."

"And who's your dad, Lord of the Vampires?" I said.

"Yes," Thorne quickly answered, shutting me up.

As Thorne explained the situation, his words took on a charismatic lilt. At first I had thought he was a stuffy old vampire, crotchety and jaded from several lifetimes of killing and sucking blood. But I quickly realized he spoke with great fervor, as if he loved words, highlighting the ones he found important and talking with an energy that surprised me.

Maybe there was something human left inside him after all.

Perhaps I shouldn't push my luck.

"Helena was dying from cancer. My father had loved her for years, but Helena didn't know our secret. It would've killed him to watch her die, but he wouldn't ask the council to approve her being turned. He'd made too many mistakes in the past and didn't want it to haunt him.

"So I did it. Without permission and knowing what I would face if I made Helena one of us. So I gladly did it and," he directed that to me, "the vampires you hate who also help serve this community came with me, deciding they would rather be with me than lose me. As I said, they can still come and go, but they choose to stay mostly."

"How thoughtful. Bloodsuckers who stick together."

My mother shot me a harsh look. "So how did Helena respond to the news that she was now a vampire?"

Thorne sipped from his sweet tea; at least that's what it looked like. "I asked her first. I made sure it was a decision she wanted. I would never turn anyone who refused."

"Well, that's very kind of you," Mama said. She glanced around at the plates. Mine and Rose's were empty. Thorne's was not. "Can I get you something else?" she asked him.

He shook his head. "No, this is wonderful. I'm finished."

She rose. "Great. If we're all done, I propose I get back to work deciphering the spell that caused the ripped shirts."

Thorne rose as well. "And I need the shirt that was taken."

"We can arrange that," Mama said. "Thorne, thank you for joining us for dinner."

He smiled. "It was my pleasure."

AFTER THORNE LEFT, I scrubbed his dishes hard to make sure none of his vampire cooties remained on them.

Mama strode by, inspecting my work. "Charming, what are you doing for the rest of the day?"

"Running to Fire Town. The bartender at the tavern said that Langdon had met up with some fire witches."

My mother shot Rose a knowing look.

"What is it?"

"Nothing," Mama sniffed. "But I wouldn't hang out with fire witches if I were you."

"Why not?"

"Because your mother's old nemesis is a fire witch," Rose said.

I quirked a brow. "Nemesis? This is the first I've heard of a *nemesis.*"

"I don't have a nemesis," my mother snapped.

"Oh? Then Frankie Firewalker isn't your nemesis?"

My eyes widened. "Who's Frankie Firewalker?"

"No one you need to concern yourself with," my mother said quickly.

"I'm intrigued."

My mother frowned at Rose. "Don't fill her head with silly ideas. Charming, I don't have a nemesis. Even if Frankie Firewalker is someone from my past, she's no enemy."

"Okay." I was unconvinced. "Does she live here?"

"Now how could Glinda's nemesis live here?" Rose said. "The magic in town is broken."

"So she doesn't," I said. "Good to know."

Mama flicked her hand toward the hallway. "And take that horrible broom with you, too. It's hideous and I don't like the way it's looking at me."

I frowned at the broom, which looked exactly as it always did. "Okay, sure. I'll take it just for you."

I snatched Broom and headed outside to find some fire witches.

It was hot. The humidity made it feel like one hundred and twenty degrees instead of ninety. I got in my car and cranked up the air-conditioning.

The way to Fire Town was marked by lots of stores I hadn't seen before: Poisoned Apple Winery—not sure if the name on that one was a hit or miss. There was also the Ole Time Witch Photo, where you and the family could dress up like witches or wizards and have your photos taken.

The kudzu wasn't as pronounced on this trek. I wondered if the fire witches zapped it back with their fiery magic.

I'd have to remember to ask.

A flock of crows met me in Fire Town. They announced my arrival with caws so loud I nearly had to cover my ears.

"Well, there went the element of surprise," I murmured sarcastically.

Fire Town itself looked as mainstream as the rest of Witch's Forge. A white clapboard sign welcomed me to Fire Town, which was one of the only reasons I knew I was in the right place.

That and the crows, that was.

A circular fire pit sat just in the center of a traffic circle. Flames like fingers reached for the sky.

I was beginning to wonder who I should to talk to when I noticed a nice little magic shop just off the road. I pulled into a parking spot, grabbed my file folder and headed inside.

Forced air cranked loudly, cooling the shop. I was fanning my blouse, trying to get some of that frigid air down my clothes, when a chipper voice greeted me.

"Welcome to Crow's Nest."

I peered around a cabinet full of curing crystals to see a red-haired, green-eyed, wide-smiling witch.

I actually smiled back. Like a genuine smile, not something I had to force.

"Hey there," I said. "Maybe you can help me."

"I can try. I don't get many shoppers, so I've got some time."

"My name's Charming Calhoun. Mayor Dixon hired me to match-make this town."

Her eyelids flared with surprise. "You're the matchmaker! Oh, I'm so excited to meet you. My name's Blaire Fireclaw."

"How do you do?"

Blaire smirked. "You haven't been here very long, have you? Living here you know not to ask how anyone's doing because everyone's magic is crap, there's no economy and if you try to leave, you can, but it still won't fix your magic."

I grimaced. "Sorry. I'm trying to change that."

Blaire shrugged. "Don't worry about it. But hey, I make truffles on the side. Want one? I just made them. I had a feeling I'd be getting in a new visitor."

I smiled and took the offer. The chocolate melted on my tongue. It was both sweet and bitter. I loved it.

"Tell me," Blaire said in a Southern twang, "did you come here to match me?"

"Actually no, but I can."

She waved her hand in dismissal. "No thanks. Not until more folks enter this town. I know all the men my age and I'm not interested in them and before you ask, I don't want to marry someone's grandfather. I don't like 'em old, neither."

I laughed. "Fair enough. But that's not why I came. You know that Langdon Huggins was murdered."

She clicked her tongue. "There's no surprise there. I'm surprised that sorry fella hadn't been knocked off earlier."

I didn't hide my surprise. "Why would you say that?"

She hiked a shoulder. "Mainly because all he ever did was stir up trouble. Langdon saw the inside of the town jail by the time he was ten."

"The *bar jail?*"

She nodded. "That's the one."

"I heard he had some friends who were fire witches."

Blaire studied me. "He did," she finally answered.

"You don't want to tell me?"

"It's a couple of witches who are always trying spells that get them in trouble with the elders."

My eyebrows shot up. "What sort of spells?"

"Oh, the usual stuff." Blaire paused to eat a truffle. The suspense was killing me. "Last year they tried putting on a fireworks show at the Fourth of July, but because no one's magic works right, the spell caused a sinkhole that nearly swallowed part of Fire Town."

Sounded like the witches I needed to meet. "Do you know if they've ever worked any sort of transformation spells?"

Blaire shrugged. "If they were trying to turn a frog into a prince, more than likely they'd end up turning a prince into an ostrich."

I laughed. "I need to talk to them. Can you tell me where I'll find these witches?"

"Sure. They run Witch Memorabilia; it's a store just down the street that's filled with figurines of famous witches and antique cauldrons and stuff."

"Perfect. Thanks."

Blaire clicked her tongue. "Let me know if you need any more help or want to sample any more truffles."

I thanked her and left. It would be good to have a friend in this town. There was no telling how long I'd be stuck here, and hanging out with my aunt and mother all the time wasn't exactly high on my priority list.

Or on my list at all, to be honest.

I found the memorabilia store easily enough and went inside. There, I found one witch and one wizard busily dusting shelves and taking inventory.

"Good afternoon," I said cheerily.

They exchanged a look before returning to their business.

Wow, tough crowd. If Witch's Forge ever opened up to outside visitors, these two would have to work on their social skills.

"I'm Charming Calhoun," I said. "The town matchmaker."

Finally the woman—a lithe and delicately boned creature with long blonde hair—turned away from the witch she was dusting with a grimy rag.

"I'm Sweet Rush and this is my twin brother, Sawyer Rush."

I said hello to both. Sweet gave me a bored stare. "What can we do for you?"

It hadn't taken me long to figure out my in. I just wasn't sure if it would work.

"I'm trying to match two people who don't seem to want to meet." I grimaced. "It's so frustrating, when you're the only person who can get two people together but they don't want anything to do with each other. I was hoping a spell could change all that."

Sawyer, who had blond hair like his sister's but wore it short and spiked on top, surveyed me with interest. "What sort of spell?"

"Oh," I said casually, studying the goods on the shelves, "something sort of like a glamour but more complicated."

"That doesn't narrow it down," Sawyer said. "Can you be more specific?"

I leaned in and lowered my voice. "I would love to be more specific, but I'm afraid what I say to y'all may get out. I'm not sure if this sort of spell is really, um, ethical."

"Oh, then please tell us what it is," Sawyer said.

I licked my lips. "Well, I've got a couple who doesn't want to meet. She wants her man to be fierce, super fierce, so I wanted to transform him into something very strong. Something so strong he might even rip out of his shirt."

Sweet narrowed her eyes. "I don't know a spell like that."

"Really?" Here went nothing. "I'm surprised because Langdon Huggins told me to ask y'all about it."

Sawyer cocked his head at me. "Langdon Huggins came to us asking about a spell, but we couldn't help him."

Sweet nodded. "He sure did. Fire magic is transformative."

"Why's that?" I said.

"Because of the nature of it," she explained. "It can destroy. But when it does, say in a forest fire, the destruction leads to rebirth. The forest regenerates when the old is lost so the new can be born."

I thought about that for a moment. "So is it possible that a spell wouldn't be needed at all for what I'm trying to do?"

"Hard to say. For sure you'd need a lot of power," Sawyer said.

"The fire springs," Sweet said. "They'd be involved in something like that, for sure."

"If that's what you're looking for," Sawyer said. "That's where you'd go, but I don't know anyone from here who could work a successful spell like that. When we couldn't help Langdon, that's where we sent him."

I wouldn't go out there by myself. I'd need to talk to my mother. She was the one studying the spell.

I thanked the twins for their help and was about to walk out the door when an idea came to me. I turned around.

"Y'all haven't heard of a witch called Frankie Firewalker, have you?" I said.

The twins exchanged a look. Sawyer answered. "We have."

I rubbed my lips in glee. "Great. Tell me everything you know."

SEVENTEEN

I headed back to discuss my progress with the mayor when a commotion in front of her office caught my attention.

A band of vampires was standing on the street. They had Cap Turner handcuffed and were dragging him away.

My jaw fell. "What the...?"

I parked the car and beelined for Thorne, who I saw standing in the middle of the melee.

I stalked up to him so angry that I was surprised my hair didn't stand on end. "What are you doing?"

He was busy guiding the men as they escorted Cap down the street. I jumped in front of the vampire, forcing him to confront me.

"What are you doing?"

He brushed past me.

Annoyed, I charged forward and grabbed his arm. "Thorne, what are you doing?"

He snatched his arm away as if my touch burned him. "What does it look like?"

"It looks like you're arresting an innocent man."

Cap's gaze dragged to me. "I didn't do it, Miss Calhoun. What they're saying I did."

"We found evidence to the contrary," Thorne said.

"What evidence?" I demanded.

"I can't share that with you," he barked.

I glared at him and folded my arms. "I'm not moving. This man is innocent."

"And how do you know that?"

"I feel it in my bones. The only way I'll move is if you pick me up yourself."

Thorne mumbled, "If you insist." The next thing I knew his arms were around me, lifting me into the air and setting me on the sidewalk.

I sighed. Well, it didn't look like I'd win this one. But Cap wasn't guilty. My gaze washed down the street until it landed on Belinda, standing off to the side.

There was no time to waste. I rushed over to her and grabbed her hands. "Belinda, listen to me. I know Cap is innocent. He didn't have anything to do with Langdon."

She sniffed in response.

"If I can prove it and he gets released, will you do me a favor?"

"What?" she said.

"Kiss him for the mayor to see?"

Belinda hesitated.

"Please," I begged. "I think you and Cap are part of the puzzle that will free this town from its present state. You could bring back Witch's Forge—the two of you with your love. Will you do it? Will you help me?"

Tears spilled from her velvety eyes. "Yes, I will."

I smiled. "Thank you." I rushed to the courthouse and raced inside. "Mama! Rose! Where are y'all?"

"In the dungeon," Rose called.

"The dungeon," I muttered. "What is she talking about?"

They weren't in the dungeon, but they were in the magic room, which my mother had now outfitted with all sorts of whips and knives.

My eyes widened as I stared at the objects. "Mama, is there something you want to tell me? Do you have some sort of fetish thing that's only now getting out to the public?"

She glared at me. "Absolutely not, Charming. I'm experimenting on ways that will rip a shirt."

"You said it was a spell."

She sniffed. "The spell might include tools."

"Okay. Weird. I have things to tell you. First, Cap was arrested for Langdon's murder."

Rose cupped her cheeks in surprise. "Not Cap."

"Yes, him. Thorne said they found evidence in his house."

"Oh, I heard about that evidence," Rose said.

I gaped at her. "How could you have heard of anything? They just arrested him."

Rose shrugged. "News travels fast. I was outside walking Pig, and Mayor Dixon said that just between us they found something in Cap's house that made it look like he could have been trying to control someone else."

"What did they find?"

"I don't know, but Cap denied it. Said he was using the thing to control his own feelings."

I groaned. "About Belinda. If he needed to control his feelings about anyone, it would be her." I slumped against the wall.

My mother and Rose gave me confused looks. Time to explain. "He loves a woman he's not supposed to, and maybe in order to quell that desire, he uses some sort of magical object to help."

"But why would Thorne arrest him if he knows we're dealing with a spell?" Mama said.

I considered that and then realized the vampire was much smarter than I gave him credit for. Something I hated to admit. "Because if he makes an arrest, whoever is guilty will think they're in the clear. They might relax, screw up."

My mother tapped her chin. "Smart thinking."

"Agreed." Then I remembered I hadn't told them the rest of what I'd learned. "I discovered a witch could use the fire springs to create the sort of spell we're looking for."

My mother considered that. "I think we should follow that lead."

I stared at Rose, shocked that my mother liked my idea. Wow. She was really getting into this whole investigation thing. I mean, first she sucked it up and broke into a vampire's house with me, and now she wanted to stake out the fire springs.

I mean, talk about a win.

Rose motioned toward Pig. "Can Pig come?"

Mama shot Rose a disdainful look. "Do you think she'll cause a ruckus?"

"Oh no, Pig wouldn't do that. She's the sweetest pig there is."

My mother gave me a skeptical look. "Pig stays here. She can come with us on our next stakeout. *If* we have one."

Rose looked disappointed, so I hugged my arm around her. "It'll be okay. Like Mama said, Pig can come next time."

"Soon as night falls, we're heading to the fire springs," my mother announced.

It could not get dark fast enough. I was on edge, feeling like we were finally closing in on what had happened to Jimmy. Maybe we'd learn the truth tonight.

I could only hope.

We loaded up into my car. My mother sat in back with the broom. "I still don't like this bristly thing. Do me a favor and set it on fire at the springs."

I shot her a dark look in the rearview. "It was a gift. Besides, you'd better be careful or it might spank you, too."

"Yes, Glinda," Rose chirped, "and gifts should be cherished."

"Not when they're hideous broomsticks. Probably has beetles living inside it."

I shook my head and followed the signs to the fire springs. We reached the entrance, which was marked by a steel sign with red lettering.

"Steel so that it doesn't burn," I remarked.

A lot with several parked cars sat off to the side.

"Park in here," my mother commanded. "We'll walk toward the back and look for a spring that isn't very obvious. And bring the broom," she commanded.

"I'm not burning it," I argued.

"I was only joking, Charming. Bring it in case we need it."

I doubted she was joking, but I did grab it. We walked quietly through the springs, which were something to witness.

They were like little ponds of fire. Every few minutes one would gurgle and spit. When the spitting got loud, a violent explosion of fire shot up from the ground, spraying into the air.

After a few sparks nearly lit my hair on fire, I learned to give the burping springs a wide berth.

"These are dangerous," Rose said. "Someone could get hurt."

"Don't get hurt," Mama said. "That's your reminder."

We found a spot where we could scan the springs from a high plateau. A few trees sprinkled our view, but for the most part it wasn't obscured.

We nestled onto the grass. Rose was slower moving, complaining that once she got down, she might not be able to get up again, but my mother quickly reminded her that we did have magic and could, in fact, help her up.

Or at least she could since my magic was limited.

We'd been staring at the springs for a few minutes when a witch approached.

"Who is that?" Rose said.

"She's got a hood on. I can't see," I said quietly.

"Maybe you can whistle and she'll lower the hood," Rose suggested.

Mama shook her head. "Just wait. Perhaps she'll lower it on her own."

The figure stepped up to the fire spring and extended her hands. The flames leaped high into the night air.

A tree rustled behind the figure. The branches bent left and right, being pushed so far I thought they might break. A moment later a creature leaped from the trees and out into the night.

Rose gasped. The thing was covered in hair from head to foot and looked more like an ape man than anything I'd ever seen.

I stared at the face for a moment, and it was only after a few seconds that I recognized the cheekbones and sharp jaw.

"Jimmy," I screamed.

Both the figure and the hairy man swirled toward me. I cringed as the man, aka Jimmy, darted across the minefield of fire springs.

The three of us glanced at each other. Fear paralyzed me as I realized my friend Jimmy was heading straight for us.

And it didn't look like he wanted to have a friendly chat.

EIGHTEEN

*J*immy was almost on us when Broom rose straight up, bristles lifted to the sky.

I opened my mouth to screech something to my mother to stop Jimmy, but the broomstick jumped into action. The handle crashed down on Jimmy's head, making him howl in pain. The brush end swiveled around and spanked Jimmy from top to bottom.

Jimmy, covered in fur and acting feral as could be, howled. Broom didn't let up until Jimmy ran from the springs, disappearing into the night.

Then the stick chased him.

In the melee, the witch disappeared into the night, and none of us knew which direction she had gone.

After a few minutes Broom returned, and then we walked back to the car. No one had said anything until we were strapped in and Broom was tucked inside.

"Well, I didn't expect that," Mama said.

"Which part? The fact that Jimmy is a hairy feral man or that the broomstick chased him away? Or was it that you froze and didn't stop Jimmy with your magic?"

I was testing her, unsure if Mama really had frozen.

132

"I didn't expect any of them," she said snidely. "But you don't have to rub it in."

I shrugged. "No one's rubbing anything in."

From the backseat Rose said, chipper as could be, "I for one am glad that Pig didn't come with us. Poor creature would've been scared to death."

I raked my fingers through my hair in frustration. "Who knows? Maybe she has secret powers we aren't aware of," I snapped. "But what happened to Jimmy? Who was that? Why would someone do that to him?"

Mama shook her head. "I didn't stop him from almost attacking us." She stared at her hands. Her face was pale, the blood drained away, and her eyes held a glassy, faraway look.

I think my mother was in shock.

Her voice was barely above a whisper. "I didn't do anything. I just saw that...*creature* coming for us and couldn't move. I was frozen."

I gently squeezed her shoulder. "We were all afraid. If it hadn't been for Broom, I don't think any of us would've survived."

She nodded, but I could tell she was numb to my words. What she needed was some sugar and female bonding.

"Come on, let's get out of here." I cranked the engine. "Who wants a root beer float?"

"Oh, I do," Rose said. "I bet Pig would love one, too."

"Great. Let's get home and make some, get our heads screwed on straight and figure out our game plan. Sound good?"

"Sounds great," Rose said enthusiastically.

My mother mumbled her agreement, but until we got some calories in her, she would be in this state.

As much as I enjoyed my mother when she wasn't flinging insults at me, I hated to see her broken.

Luckily sugar was a great cure.

A little while later we sat around the kitchen, scoops of ice cream sitting in tall glasses.

With one hand on the fridge door I said nicely, "House, can we have some root beer?"

A moment later I opened the door and there sat a gallon of Barq's. "Classy. The house has taste. No knock-off brands for us." I poured the fizzy drink into the glasses and waited for the bubbles to recede before topping each off.

I sat and faced my mother and aunt. Rose was already nibbling ice cream from her spoon when I dipped mine in and brought back a creamy, soda-filled treat.

The sweet ice cream and tangy root beer hit my tongue. I moaned. "Oh, that is what we need. Mama, you have to eat. It'll help."

"I don't know what got into me."

I pointed my spoon at her. "What got into you was that you were being attacked by a creature that used to be human. We need to know what spell did that and who's controlling it."

She sat listlessly. I snapped my fingers in front of her. "In the words of Cher in *Moonstruck*, 'Snap out of it!' Get a grip. For goodness' sake, you're Glinda Calhoun. Half the witches in the world want to be you, and you're acting like you died. You didn't. None of us did. Now do us all a favor and figure out the spell. You're the best person for the job."

Mama exhaled a deep shot of air and slowly lifted her spoon. She dipped it in the float and took a small bite. "Thank you for making this, Charming," she said in her usual voice dripping with smugness.

I smiled. Mama was back. Great. Now we could get to business. "So Jimmy isn't dead. He's been transformed into some sort of hairy ape creature."

"It's a Bigfoot spell," Mama said matter-of-factly.

"A Bigfoot spell? I've never heard of such a thing."

"Oh, they used to be all the rage," Rose explained. "But then they fell out of fashion when the space age became popular. Then folks started looking into alien spells."

My head swam with confusion. "I don't understand any of that."

"Bigfoot sightings are usually attributed to witches," Mama explained in human speak, something Rose was incapable of. "Whenever a person claims to have seen Bigfoot it's usually a witch who's worked the spell."

"Is it a spell or a curse?" I questioned. "Jimmy isn't going along with it of his own free will, I can promise you that."

She patted my hand and gave it a squeeze. "At least he's safe."

"For now," Rose said. "But we've seen him as the creature, and the witch knows we saw him."

The room quieted. I closed my eyes. "This is so bad."

"Let me go back and explain the spell," Mama said. "Bigfoot spells are control spells, that's for sure. Why would a witch do that? Either to make a person do what they want by controlling an individual, or perhaps the witch wanted to get something done and couldn't do it themselves or else they'd be caught. So they created a Bigfoot to do their dirty work for them."

"Neither of those are good," I said. "Both involve controlling someone."

"That's exactly right." Rose licked ice cream from her spoon. "We're talking about true evil. There's a lot of that in the world."

I turned back to Mama. "Tell me more."

She brushed her hair back from her face. "There isn't much to say because we don't know which witch is in control of Jimmy and we don't know why the witch spelled him. Two things working against us."

"But it was the same witch who placed the spell on Langdon. Yet when he died, he was human." Then I remembered the long hair I had found on Langdon's body. "But he had a hair on him, like a really long one. Could it have been one from when he was a Bigfoot?"

"Perhaps," Mama said, her eyes narrowing, "Langdon was black-mailing the witch. When she lifted the spell, Langdon remembered what she had done to him and he was using that against her. So she had him killed."

I groaned. "What if it's even worse than that?"

Rose's gaze darted from Pig, who she was currently feeding ice cream float to under the table, back to me. "What do you mean?"

"What if Jimmy did it?"

Mama grimaced. "That does complicate things. Jimmy would be highly dangerous. Exceedingly dangerous."

"He already tried to attack us," I said. "The person I know inside Jimmy isn't there. He's been taken over. We have to save him."

"In order to do that, we first have to know who cast the spell," she said. "Until we figure out the witch behind it, we're powerless."

I sighed. "But now the witch knows we're on to her. She won't be easy to catch."

"Someone in town must know something," Mama said. "Or at least have their suspicions."

A thought occurred to me and I gasped. "What if now that the witch knows we know, what if she decides to get rid of Jimmy? As long as he's around, he can lead people back to her. It's in her best interest to kill him."

Rose grimaced. "I hate to say it, but I think you're right, Charming."

Mama nodded in agreement. "Then we just have to find the witch before she can do that. I don't think she got a good look at us." A spark lit in my mother's eyes. "Which means, Charming, that you're free to walk about Fire Town and hand out your matchmaking questionnaires."

I frowned. "Why would that help us?"

"Because it not only gives you a reason to snoop around the Fire Town, it will help us look for ingredients that might have been used in the spell."

"What sort of ingredients?"

Mama snapped her fingers, and the book from her magic room appeared on the table, open to the very center. She thumbed through it while Pig snorted happily. Pig now sat in Rose's lap greedily licking the float.

"You realize you're teaching Pig bad habits," I scolded.

Rose scratched Pig behind the ears. "She's thirsty, and if you were thirsty, I'd give you a float."

"I'm not a pig."

"Even if you were, I'd offer you the option."

"I found it," Mama said, interrupting our ridiculous conversation.

"Found what?" I asked.

She tapped a fingernail in the book. "The Bigfoot spell."

I peered over the table, trying to get a look. "Is it called that?"

"Well no, not exactly, but it's the same basic principle."

"What's it called?"

"Why does it matter?" she said, exasperated.

"In case anyone mentions it, I want to know what it is."

"Fine." She released a heavy sigh. "It's called Animal Transformation Spell."

"Pretty vague."

"You asked," she snapped. Mama pushed aside a lock of hair that had fallen into her eyes. "The things you need for this spell are mandrake root, blood and milk."

"Oh wow. Well, it looks like that should be easy to track down," I said sarcastically. "I barely know what a mandrake looks like, every house will have milk and we're all full of blood. It's not like someone's going to walk around carrying a vial of the stuff."

My mother shot me a dark look. I shrank back. "That's what's required. It also says anyone who's under the influence of the spell may appear to have a cold."

I quirked a skeptical brow at her.

"That's what it says," Mama said snidely.

"When they're a Bigfoot they'll have a cold? That doesn't make sense."

Mama sighed, obviously frustrated with my question. "No. Some who are cursed can transform back to human, but not all."

"What does that depend on?" I asked.

"The depth of the curse."

I frowned. "So Langdon had turned back to human but if he had been a Bigfoot does that mean he wasn't as deeply cursed?"

She shrugged. "That or the curse was revoked."

I shook my head. "This is a wild-goose chase."

She shot me another harsh look.

"Okay. Okay. I'll hand out my questionnaires in Fire Town tomorrow. I'll see if anyone has any mandrake. I'll ask who keeps gigantic vials of blood in their basements."

My mother closed the tome. "I don't need your sarcasm. Rose and I will be working, too."

"We will?" Rose said.

"Yes, we need to see if we can discover a generic cure spell, though I have the feeling that unless we know who is behind it, we won't get very far."

She tapped her teeth. "You'll need to work fast, Charming."

"I know. I've got to save Jimmy. That's what I've been trying to do."

My mother shook her head. "I'm afraid you don't understand. The transformation spell, if allowed to go on for too long, can cause irreparable damage to the person afflicted by it."

I knotted the bottom of my shirt. I had the feeling I wasn't going to like where this was headed. "What sort of damage?"

My mother's piercing aqua eyes landed on me, causing a shiver to ripple down my spine. "The spell will lead to death."

NINETEEN

"*E*xtra! Extra! Come get your matchmaking questionnaires! Find your soul mate today! Or tomorrow! Soon! Find your soul mate soon!"

I stood in the middle of Fire Town like a newsie shouting for folks to come and take my questionnaire so I could help them find true love.

As stupid as this was, it actually accomplished two tasks. The first was that it proved to me that every fire witch with the exception of maybe one or two was supposed to pair up with a wizard of opposite power.

The other thing it did was let me meet pretty much every inhabitant in town.

"Charming!"

The voice came from behind me. I turned around, a big fat smile on my face—because I had to look like I was having the time of my life while tracking down whoever had cursed Jimmy. I was met with the matching smile of Mayor Winnifred Dixon. Her assistant, Emily, followed behind her.

"Mayor Dixon, have you thought about what I said about the law?"

She dismissed my question with a wave. "Proof, Charming. I need proof."

"I'm working on it."

"Have you heard anything from your man Jimmy?"

I glanced around to make sure no one could hear me. "Actually, I have."

The mayor's eyes widened with interest. She pressed her meaty fingers together. "What's that?"

I leaned in. "Just between us, I saw Jimmy last night. He's been transformed into a Bigfoot."

The mayor sucked air. Emily's eyes popped to saucers. "No!" The mayor gasped. "We haven't had a Bigfoot sighting in years."

"It's true. He attacked my family. I'm afraid Jimmy may be dangerous, but please, keep this between us. We're trying to figure out a way to help him and find the witch who did this. You wouldn't know anyone who's into that sort of thing, would you?"

The mayor sounded insulted that I'd even asked her. "No, of course not. Emily?"

Emily shoved her glasses up her nose. "No, no one I know would dabble in any sort of magic like that. It's horrible."

"Whoever it is," I added, "would need mandrake. Do you know where they might have procured mandrake?"

Mayor Dixon rubbed her chin. "Perhaps behind the falls."

"I'm sorry?"

"You drove through the falls to enter Witch's Forge. There's a pull off right before you leave and a cavern behind the falls. It's been rumored mandrake grows there."

"Good to know."

Mayor Dixon squeezed my arm. "Charming, be careful. I don't like the idea of a Bigfoot on the loose."

I shivered. "Me neither."

They left and I handed out a few more questionnaires, but I was more interested in looking around at the mandrake roots under the falls to see if the witch who was controlling Jimmy would go out there, or if she had left any clues as to who she was.

I set out alone later that afternoon. I did take Broom with me, but I managed to slip out of the house without my mother or Rose figuring out what I was doing. They had work to do, and besides, I didn't want them worrying about me.

I found the pull off easily enough. I didn't want to park at it because my car could be spotted by someone, so I drove it down the road and then hid it behind a sign thanking folks for visiting Witch's Forge.

The cave was chilly. Very chilly. Like a good fifteen degrees cooler than outside. Probably had to do with the water rushing over the falls and plunging into some sort of magical vortex, but I wasn't complaining.

The walls were smooth and brown. The floor was dirt, and sprouting up were little green plants that looked like the tops of turnips.

Though I was tempted to pull one out, I was also afraid the mandrake would scream, so I left them alone. I'd just peered around the back of the cave when I heard someone pulling up outside.

I darted into a dark nook and waited. It was still daylight, so I could see just fine.

A witch entered the cave, her head down. She beelined straight for a root and sang a song. Then she plucked it from the dirt.

The thing looked human. It really did. The root had arms and legs and even a head with a knotted root face that reminded me of an old man's features.

The witch wrapped the root in a towel and left. I quickly followed, getting a good look at the vehicle—a dark blue Honda sedan.

As soon as the car headed toward town, I sprinted to my car, started her up and followed. I caught up fast but kept my distance.

The car turned down the path to Earth Town. I frowned. That didn't make any sense. Shouldn't we have been going to Fire Town?

I followed until the car stopped in front of a house that I recognized. I watched as the witch, her back still to me, got out of the car and entered the home.

I nearly catapulted from my vehicle before I sprinted across the grass. The windows were open, and I watched as the woman headed to a back room. She pulled something out from under the bed—a dish —and added the mandrake to it.

She finished her work and shoved the dish back under the bed. When she glanced up, our eyes met. My breath caught in the back of my throat, tickling a sensitive place and causing me to cough.

"Belinda," I croaked.

Her eyelids flared. "Charming!"

After what felt like a lifetime of seconds I stopped hacking. My stomach hurt from coughing, and my throat was raw. I swallowed to ease the pain, but it didn't do much good.

Belinda reached out the window. "You didn't see me here."

"I did see you. You're putting a spell on someone. It's obvious."

"No!" Her lower lip trembled, and tears spilled down her cheeks. "You don't understand. I'm not hurting anyone. Cap asked me to do this."

I paused. Something rang true in her words. "What?"

She made a stop gesture with her hands. "Wait just a minute. I'll be right out."

We found a park bench to sit on in the residential section of Earth Town. A brisk breeze lifted the hair off the back of my neck, and I smiled at how delicious it felt.

"Why were you in Cap's house?"

Belinda nibbled her bottom lip. "He's been using the mandrake on a spell that stops him from caring about me."

I cringed but already knew it was true. "That's horrible—to force himself to stop caring."

She shook her head. Dark curls spiraled around her face. "No it isn't. It makes life so much easier if we don't care about each other, and the mandrake here is still potent, unaffected by the town, so the spell works."

"But why wouldn't you want to be togeth—oh, wait. The town's law that makes the two of you being together illegal. That's why."

She nodded. Tears dripped off her chin and splashed onto her lap. "We couldn't be together, so he started using the mandrake. But the police found the last mandrake and confiscated it. It's what they arrested him for. I was replacing it so that he wouldn't have to suffer while he's at the jail."

I squeezed her hand and did my best to smile kindly. "I will make sure you and Cap can be together, and I will help turn this town around. I promise you that."

Wow. Could I promise that? Seemed like I was trying to fill a tall order, but this town needed me. This town needed Southern Belles and Spells Matchmakers.

It needed me more than it knew.

"Do you know of anyone else who uses mandrake?"

Belinda swiped a tissue under her sniffling nose. "The only other person I know is Sweet Rush."

I clicked my tongue in interest. "The twin who runs the figurine store in Fire Town?"

Belinda nodded. "Sweet has always been into strange things. She and her brother once promised that the town would one day thank them for saving it. It was winter and we were in the middle of a blizzard. They used their magic to try to help the town, but only ended up making the blizzard worse and calling down mosquitoes who could survive the cold."

"That's what happens when you use magic in a town that's known for its power being broken," I commented.

"Yeah," she said. "There may be other witches who use the mandrakes, but Sweet's the only person I know who's actually used one in a spell."

And who apparently wanted some sort of town appreciation. Wouldn't she get town appreciation if she, say, created a monster and then saved the town from it?

Sounded like a plausible theory, one I should probably tell the police.

I thanked Belinda and left, heading back. I decided to stop at the jail first, to see if Thorne was in.

I arrived as the sun was setting. I headed straight inside the bar and was confronted with the gang from the first night.

AMY BOYLES

I rolled my eyes. "It's not even dark yet. Don't y'all have someplace better to be? At least until it's completely pitch outside?"

Peek, the Carhart-wearing vampire, smirked. "You got a wish to be in jail, little miss?"

I fisted my hand to my hip and shot the vampire the meanest glare I could think of. "I'm here to see your boss. Where's Thorne?"

"Out." Peek's gaze flickered to my throat. "Maybe we can help. You got a problem that the police can fix?"

I squinted at him, trying to figure out if he meant that honestly or if Peek was being sarcastic.

"Are you joking?"

He shook his head. "No. You're in the police station. We do help people."

"And here I thought all y'all did was intimidate everyone who walked in and stared at their necks as if you were deciding whether or not they were a tasty treat."

"We do that, too."

I bristled. "No thanks. I don't need your help. I'll wait for Thorne outside."

I left the Flying Hickory Stick and stood outside. I inhaled deeply, drinking in the air. All those vampires made my heart race, set my pulse in a flutter. I hadn't let my body feel fear in a long time.

Fear was not a place I lived in. My life's work was to make people happy, to bring them together. It wasn't to be afraid of anything.

"What are you doing out here?"

"Ah!"

I flinched, annoyed with myself for being frightened. I glanced over. Thorne's outline loomed in the darkness. For the first time I noticed there weren't a lot of streetlamps by the tavern.

"What are you doing out here?" he repeated.

"I'm looking for you."

His voice was harsh, cold. The sound of it was like a steel rod being driven into my spine. "Trying to make more of a mess than you already have of my investigation?"

"What are you talking about?"

144

He approached. His silvery eyes flashed with anger, but the deep scowl on his face made Thorne look more handsome.

Wait. Scratch that. This vampire was not handsome. He was lethal, dangerous.

Thorne didn't stop until he stood six inches from my chest. Then he reached behind me.

The distinct smell of him wafted up my nose. I would've thought vampires would smell of death and dirt, but Thorne proved that theory wrong.

Something ripped behind me. I jumped.

Of course the vampire didn't flinch. He thrust something under my nose. I shrank back, a stupid gut response to his movements.

The last thing I wanted was for this vampire to think I was afraid of him.

I was not.

Okay, maybe I was a little.

I peered at the sheet. "What is that?"

"What does it look like?" he snapped.

"A wanted poster."

"It is. Look closer."

Thorne held the paper so I could grab it. I stared at the picture. A sketch of a typical Bigfoot was on it, and the word WANTED was typed above the sketch.

Oh no. I realized what had happened. Word had gotten out about me and my family seeing Jimmy, and someone had made these and posted them.

I groaned. "I'm sorry. I guess this is my fault."

Thorne nodded. "At least you have the sense to admit this is your fault."

His words needled me to the core. "Look, I said I'm sorry. There's no need to insult my intelligence."

Anger flared in his eyes. "You just ruined my entire investigation."

"An investigation where you've got the wrong person in jail—on purpose," I shot back.

Thorne seemed to grow angrier, which made him appear even larger. "You and your family need to stay out of my way."

"Me and my family are the only ones figuring out what's going on in Witch's Forge."

"You need to stop!"

I poked his chest. "You need to do a better job' policing."

A crash that sounded like a trash can falling over jarred us from our argument.

Thorne paused.

"Jimmy," I said. "I bet that's him."

Thorne shot me a look full of warning. "Stay here."

I smirked. "The heck I am. That's my friend out there. If you're going, I'm going with you—"

But Thorne was already gone, running in a flash down the street.

I ground my teeth and kicked up my heels in a run. I'd be darned if I was going to let that vampire catch my friend without me there.

I set off right behind him to catch Jimmy, the Bigfoot.

TWENTY

*W*hoever said keeping up with a vampire was easy was a liar. Actually I'm pretty sure no one ever said that—in all of history. Thorne was a blur, disappearing into the night within seconds.

Luckily I had exceptional hearing, if I did say so myself. I quickly tracked down the sound and found Thorne in an alley.

"Where is he?"

The vampire whirled on me. "What are you doing? I told you to stay back."

I thrust out my hip to show how sassy I could be. He glared at me as if he didn't care. "We're talking about my friend. I don't want you to get your vampire claws on Jimmy and hurt him."

He scoffed. "Please. Your friend probably killed Langdon."

"What?" I screeched. Something hissed behind me. I turned around right as an aluminum trash can, that for some reason was sitting atop a dumpster, crashed down, hitting me hard across the knuckles of my right hand.

"Ow!"

Thorne rushed to my side. He took a protective stance as a cat sprinted down from the dumpster and scampered away.

I shook out my hand, which only made the pain worse. "Darn cat! And why was that trash can on top of a dumpster? Who would do that? Why would they do that? Ow, it really hurts."

Thorne frowned. "Let me see it."

I cradled my hand. "No. It might be bleeding. It could put you into a frenzy."

"It's not bleeding," he argued.

"How do you know?"

"Because I'm like a shark," he said pointedly. "I can smell blood up to a mile away."

"Oh," I said quietly.

"Let me see it."

I studied him, unsure of his motives. "Are you going to make it worse?"

"Why would I do that?"

"Because you don't like me."

"I don't want you harmed. You could sue the police department."

I rolled my eyes and showed him my hand.

"The knuckles are puffy. Let's get you some ice."

"I don't need ice from you."

"Would you can it?" he said. "I'm trying to help and all you're doing is spitting in my face. Now, are you right-handed?"

"Yes," I said softly.

"Do you want to be able to write tomorrow?"

Yes. "No."

He shook his head. Dark hair swam over his cheekbones before receding back into place. "I'll take that as a yes. Come on. Let's get you fixed up."

"Where are we going? Not the tavern?"

"No. My house. You won't be bothered there. Besides, wouldn't you like to see it when you're not sneaking around at night?"

Yes. "No."

"Come on. I'll drive you."

"I'll follow you. How's that?"

He shrugged. "Suit yourself."

Thorne drove a pickup truck. No, I'm not kidding. I was shocked. I thought for sure he'd drive something like a Jaguar or a Bentley, but no, he drove a regular Japanese imported pickup.

This vampire was full of surprises, but one thing he was right about, if I didn't get ice on my hand and fast, it would be so swollen the next day I wouldn't be able to do anything.

By the time we reached the house, my hand throbbed and it was two sizes too big.

Thorne took one look and grimaced. "Come on."

We walked in. He turned on the gas lamps, threw his keys on a table and led me to the kitchen.

He grabbed a tea towel and dumped ice from the freezer into it. With the gentleness of a lover, Thorne took my hand and rested the bag atop it.

I shivered. I wasn't sure if it was the ice or his touch, which was warmer than I expected.

Thorne released me, crossed to a fireplace and turned a knob until a gas fire roared.

"That should warm you up," he said quietly.

As much as I didn't want to say it, I felt I owed it to Thorne to say, "Thank you."

"You're welcome."

He sat in the chair opposite me, in front of the fireplace in his cozy kitchen. I had no idea what to say. I was sitting in a vampire's kitchen, a room they don't even technically need, treating my hand.

After a moment he glanced over. "I'll tell you something if you tell me something."

"What's the something?"

"Ah, ah." A sly smile danced on his lips. "You have to agree to the game first."

I sniffed. "I don't like those terms."

"They're the only terms I'm giving you." His gaze pierced me. His silvery eyes held a note of mischief I hadn't seen in Thorne before. I kinda liked it.

He leaned over. "I can promise you that you will like the information you receive. But you have to trust me."

I pulled away. "I don't trust vampires."

"Maybe you should start."

"Maybe I shouldn't."

He nodded and sat back, his face unreadable. What was this? Him playing some sort of pity card that I couldn't decipher? I did not pity vamps.

"How's your hand?"

"Better."

Ugh. Was he going to guilt me into playing? Just figured. I sighed and, against my better judgment, relented.

"Okay, I'll play."

"Why do you hate vampires?"

"Because when I was a child I was attacked by one. Now. What've you got to tell me?"

He shot me a dark look. "That's barely scratching the surface. Tell me more."

My gaze darted from him to the fire and to my hand, which didn't throb nearly as much now that the cold was biting into my flesh.

The only real people I had to talk to were my mom and aunt. What could it hurt to have someone else to tell a story to?

I rubbed my eyes with the opposite hand and sighed. "When I was young, I was at home, sleeping. My father was the only other person in the house. It was late; I was in bed. A vampire snuck into my room and attacked me.

"The creature's bite woke me up. I screamed. To this day I still can't believe I woke up."

"You never should have," he murmured. "Vampires are creatures of stealth."

"I know." I sneaked a glance at him, but Thorne's face was unreadable. "But I did. My father rushed into the room and fought the vampire, killing it, but not before the bloodsucker got in a few blows of his own."

My voice caught. I hadn't thought about the details of this story in a long, long time. I exhaled and finished. "My father died from the wounds. He was so tired, and he should've helped himself. He could've healed his flesh and lived, but he couldn't save both of us."

"And you were hurt badly." Thorne stared into the fire as he spoke. "Too badly to survive otherwise."

I nodded. "My father gave his life for mine." I pulled my shirt collar down to reveal two small puncture wounds. The skin was puckered now, healed, but the scars would always remain.

"They still itch at times—like when I'm angry or afraid."

He nodded in understanding. "It's an after effect of our venom. As long as you're alive it will probably always itch." He paused and stared at the fire. "Your mother doesn't seem to hate my kind like you."

I smirked. "She's better at understanding that it was only one vampire that killed my father and not *every* vampire." My gaze leveled on him. "I, on the other hand, have issues."

"I'm sorry," he said quietly. "I don't blame you for hating my kind."

"Thank you," I said.

He looked up, surprised by my words. For the first time since I'd met Thorne, I smiled at him. His lips slowly curved upward, and our smiles lingered, melting some of the icy barrier built up around us.

"Now you," I said.

"You're eyes are very violet."

I rolled them. "That better not be what you were going to tell me."

He shook his head. "It isn't. You may not realize this, but Witch's Forge has a history of Bigfoot sightings."

"I've heard a bit about that."

"I was aware of this and wanted to keep the knowledge of what Langdon and Jimmy had become silent."

"I thought you didn't know," I argued.

"I had my suspicions, but there were no eyewitnesses."

"Until me and my family." I realized what he was alluding to. "And I told the mayor, who in turn told everyone." I cringed. "I'm sorry."

"This could create hysteria. Plus, the witch involved knows we are aware of what he or she did."

"So I just made your job harder."

"I'm afraid so."

"How can I make it up to you?" I squeaked. But even before the words were out of my mouth, I knew what Thorne would say.

"Stay out of it. For your own safety."

"You'd be better served if I helped you."

Thorne chuckled. That ticked me off. Sure, I wasn't the most powerful witch. I didn't even really care about magic. I had my calculations and that was enough for me, but for Thorne to flat-out laugh in my face was frustrating.

I bristled. My voice became steely cold as I glared at him. "You don't have to make fun of me."

"I'm not." He pressed a hand to his breast as if to prove how earnest he could be. "I wasn't laughing because you suggested you help. I was laughing because I can't see your aunt and pig tracking down a killer."

I folded my arms. "You never know what those two might track down."

He turned back to the fire as if to shut down the entire conversation. "How's your hand?"

Okay, I guess he was actually shutting down the conversation. "It's good. Better. Thank you."

"I'm not a healer, but I know that a little cold will help those knuckles."

I dared to shoot the vampire a smile even though I was afraid the simple gesture would make me lose my soul to him or something. His gaze flickered over me, and I felt myself drawn to him as if Thorne Blackstock was a magnet and I was...well, the other half of a magnet.

"You know you could use me. Maybe Jimmy is still inside there somewhere—still in the creature he's become. He might just need a little talking to, something that will help snap him out of whatever spell he's under. What do you say?"

Thorne scowled. "You're missing a very important point. He attacked you. I'm afraid you're not the first person he's attacked. There *is* something good that's come from all the posters being put up about him—people will be aware of his presence. Hopefully that will stop another attack."

"*Another* attack?"

He nodded, his gaze leveled on me. My stomach quivered. My pulse quickened, and I realized what Thorne was saying.

"You think he killed Langdon."

"I think it's a possibility. Now that we have a verified sighting of the creature, my men and I will go out and hunt him tonight."

I grimaced. "You won't kill him, will you?"

"Charming"—my name on his lips sent a cold shiver racing straight to my heart—"we will do whatever we have to in order to bring Jimmy in. If it means killing him, then that's what we'll do. I don't want that, but he's dangerous."

I couldn't argue with Thorne. He was right. Jimmy could be a killer. But in my heart I felt that he wasn't. Sure, he'd run toward my family, but no one had been hurt. No one had been killed.

But send a mess of bloodsuckers after Jimmy and I doubted he'd make it out alive.

If I wanted to save my friend, there was only one choice—I had to find Jimmy first, before Thorne.

I plastered on a wide smile. "Good luck. I hope you find him."

TWENTY-ONE

$\mathcal{A}$fter I left Thorne's manor home, I headed over to the mayor's office to see if she was in. It was getting late, so chances were that she'd gone home, but I needed more details about her meeting with Jimmy that never happened.

I found the mayor at her desk. Emily was bustling around, busy on the phone fielding calls about the Bigfoot.

"Yes, we've had one confirmed sighting. No, there's no reason to think the creature will attack you in your house." Poor girl sounded exasperated.

Mayor Dixon thumbed toward Emily. "She's the best person to deal with the public about the creature. Comes from a family of Bigfoot hunters."

I angled my jaw up at that comment. "Bigfoot hunters?"

"Yes," Emily answered after hanging up the phone. "My family were some of the first settlers here and they hunted them down. Caused some problems with a few of the natives. Supposedly they put a curse on my family." She laughed nervously. "The type that means we won't thrive, but here I am. Safe and sound."

"Interesting. Mayor, I believe Jimmy was supposed to meet with you the morning he disappeared."

She pulled her compact from her purse, flipped it open and applied a coat of powder to her nose. "He was supposed to and didn't, you have it right."

"Did he call? Say anything was amiss?"

The mayor blotted her lips on a tissue and smiled into the mirror. She rubbed away a line of red staining her teeth. "No, I don't believe so. I had spoken to him before and he said he was checking into the matches, that something wasn't right, but that was all. Then he didn't show up. I only got worried later in the day when Emily tried calling him and he never answered."

I tapped a finger against my file folder and rose from my chair. "Thank y'all for your time. I appreciate it."

Before I exited the office, Mayor Dixon called me back. "Charming?"

"Yes?"

"Be sure to lock your door tonight. You never know what that Bigfoot might be capable of."

I nodded my thanks and left. When I reached the house, I found my aunt in the parlor surrounded by a dozen potted plants.

"What's all this?"

"Charming, you're just in time. Your mother is having me grow herbs for her magic." She handed me a watering jug. "Would you be a dear and fetch more water?"

"Sure."

Pig snorted happily as I passed her. "Hello, Pig." The little potbellied roly-poly of an animal brushed up against Broom, who seemed content rubbing its bristles over Pig's back.

"Looks like y'all two are getting along," I murmured.

I found Mama in the kitchen, pouring over her book of magic. "Oh, you're home," she said flatly.

"Good to see you, too," I muttered. I flipped on the faucet and filled the jug. "We have a problem."

"Worse than a Bigfoot in a town like Witch's Forge?" she said over her shoulder. "My power hasn't started to dwindle, but there's no telling if whatever cursed this place will start to affect me."

155

I turned off the faucet and settled the jug on the counter. "The whole town knows about Bigfoot."

"Yes, thank you for keeping it a secret, Charming."

"I didn't realize it was."

Her eyes narrowed. "How could it not be? Telling people—even witches—that there's a mythological creature on the loose is like lighting a stick of dynamite and throwing it in a pond."

"What? It'll explode?" I said.

"Yes," she said sharply, "and kill off half the fish."

Her logic confused me. "Are you saying I'm killing fish? Or that the town is exploding?"

"I'm saying you're causing a problem," Mama snapped.

"I was only trying to help." I raised my hand to stop any more arguments. "Look, the vampire police are searching for Jimmy tonight. If they find him, there's a good chance that they'll take him in dead rather than alive."

She sucked air. "Did Thorne tell you that?"

"He did."

Mama arched a perfectly plucked brow. "My, my. You two are getting cozy."

I kept my tone curt to shut down any further discussion of the topic. "We're not getting anything, but he did tell me about the hunt." I glanced at my watch. "They must be leaving soon."

"They must."

She didn't make a move to leave. "We have to find Jimmy," I pleaded. "Before they do."

"And do what? How will we stop him? I don't have a spell that will do anything."

I stared at her in disbelief. "But you're the great Glinda Calhoun. You created a wall of water, surely you can figure out something that will help Jimmy. Mama," I said slowly, "they think he killed Langdon."

"Impossible. That man doesn't have a mean bone in his body."

"Who doesn't?" Rose's head popped in the doorway. "Sorry to butt in, but Charming was taking an awful long time with the water."

"Jimmy doesn't," I explained. "He's a gentle person, but now the vampire police are hunting him tonight and we need to help. The vamps might hurt, even kill, him if they think he's a threat."

Mama threw her hands in the air. "I don't know how to catch a Bigfoot."

"I do," Rose said quietly.

I exchanged a curious look with my mother before directing to Rose, "You do?"

"Well of course, silly. Everyone knows if you want to attract a Bigfoot, all you have to do is hang your panties out in the forest."

I rubbed my lips together, trying to form a coherent thought in my head. Shockingly, nothing came to me.

"You do?" I said.

She nodded. "Of course. All Bigfoots are pulled by their primal urges. They want to procreate same as any man. So, hanging panties will do the trick every time."

I shrugged my shoulders. Mama grabbed her purse. "Well, what are we waiting for? Grab your panties, Charming."

"Me?" How horrifying. "You want me use my panties?"

She gave me an icy look. "Who else's?"

"Yours."

"I have an older body. We need someone young, like you."

Ugh. This was getting more hideous as we talked about it. "All I have are clean panties."

Rose clapped her hands. "What did you think? We'd hang dirty underwear? Absolutely not. Only the clean ones will do."

I grumbled as I marched up the stairs to empty a few panties from my drawer. I grabbed three and was about to head back down when Rose shouted up, "Get all you can. We need them!"

I mumbled something inappropriate about family and swiped every last clean undie from the drawer. I was about to go outside when Jimmy's calendar fell to my feet. Apparently the house thought I needed to give it another gander.

I glared up at the ceiling. "Not you, too," I said to the house.

The house did not reply.

I picked it up and tucked it under my arm. The five of us—me, Rose, Mama, Pig and Broom—loaded up into my car.

"Why'd you bring Pig and Broom?" I asked Rose.

"Because they get along well."

"I'll drive," Mama said. "I may not know everything about this town, but I know how to get to the boonies."

"Fine by me."

As Mama drove, I opened the calendar, trying to retrace Jimmy's steps. Who could he have met that turned him this way?

I found the entry where he'd written *LH* and *BF*. I stared at the words until it hit me.

"Oh my gosh! I've been so stupid."

"Why's that?" Mama said.

I shook my head, cursing under my breath. "Jimmy wrote LH and BF. When I first saw this, I thought Jimmy had gotten Belinda's second initial wrong. Her last name is Ogle and I didn't understand about the F. But now I get it."

"Get what?" Rose said.

I turned around where I could see her. "The BF isn't Belinda's incorrect initials. It stands for Bigfoot. Jimmy knew Langdon was a Bigfoot. He knew and he also must've known who had turned Langdon; that's why Jimmy is in this mess. That's why he was turned into one of the creatures."

"Yes, but who did it?" Mama said.

I considered the question. "That's what I don't know. All I know for sure is that Jimmy was supposed to show up to the mayor's office one morning, but then he vanished. There are no witnesses. Mama, that's why we have to catch him and turn him back into a human."

"I've told you I can't do that without knowing who the witch was who turned him in the first place."

"We know the witch who turned Jimmy still keeps in contact with him. We saw her at the fire springs."

"Sounds to me like if you want to know something, you should be asking the mayor's office," Rose said. "They seem to know just about everything that's going on in this town."

I snorted. "That's the truth. Emily, the mayor's assistant, comes from a long line of Bigfoot hunters. Maybe we should swing by her house and see if she'll help us."

"Why don't we just get some of her panties," Rose offered. "That way we'll have plenty to lure the Bigfoot away from the vampires."

"Did this Emily say she was going to hunt for the Bigfoot?" Mama said.

I shook my head. "No. In fact, she was coughing up a storm the other day, almost as if she was about to hack up half a lung."

The cabin grew silent. I dragged my gaze from the road to my mother. "Are you thinking what I'm thinking?"

"That Pig is hungry?" Rose said.

I shook my head. "Oh my gosh. It's so obvious. The coughing! Mama, you said coughing was a symptom of the spell. Emily! She's the one that turned Jimmy into a Bigfoot!"

"And she changes herself," Mama said.

"She was there the night Langdon was murdered." Energy coursed through me. Why hadn't I put this together before? "Emily had access to Langdon. By why did she turn him into a Bigfoot?"

"Perhaps she wants to save the town on her own," Mama suggested.

"And Jimmy was a monkey wrench in that plan." My voice filled with wonder. "And somehow Jimmy figured out that Langdon had been a Bigfoot but was now back to being human. Langdon didn't seem very smart. Heck, he might've let it slip when Jimmy was trying to match him up with Belinda. Langdon probably told him about Emily, and then Jimmy confronted her."

My mother's gaze met mine. "So she changed him." A smile curled on her face. "Isn't it fun working together?"

It was hard not to admit it. "Yes. So Emily's the murderer, and if she's a Bigfoot too, she might be hard to stop."

"I don't think you're realizing the worst part," Rose said. "What if she wants to mate with Jimmy and create a whole bunch of little Bigfoots?"

"Ew. Mama, you'd better haul some butt. We've got a mating ritual to stop."

Mama ground down on the accelerator, and I was thrown back into my seat. Pig squealed and Broom rustled against Pig's face. Pig snapped at Broom, grabbing it by the bristles.

A spark lit on the stick. I grabbed hold of it to stop Pig and Broom from setting the car on fire.

The spark unrolled like a ribbon and snaked up my arm. I shot a frantic look to my mother.

"What's happening?"

She craned her neck to see magic unwinding like kudzu roping up my bicep.

She released a disgusted breath. "Well, Charming, it looks like the prophecy is starting. Great timing. Just when we're about to catch a Bigfoot."

"The prophecy where I lose all my magic?"

In that moment I realized I didn't want to lose all my magic. Yes, I barely had any, but I didn't want it to leave me.

Mama stopped the car. The tires kicked up a fog of dust that encircled us.

She threw the gearshift into park. "No, not that prophecy. The prophecy where you gain all your powers."

"What?" I said.

Rose pulled Broom away from me. "Charming, there's something we need to tell you."

TWENTY-TWO

*M*agic roped around my arm. I jumped out of the car and brushed it away, but the power glowed.

"What do you mean?" I fumed. "What is this about the prophecy, and why are you both still sitting in the car? Why aren't you getting out and helping me?"

My mother and Rose slowly exited my Cooper. Gravel crunched beneath my mother's heels. She surveyed me as if I were a project—as if adding a different color eyeshadow to my lids would change something about me.

"Does it hurt?" my mother asked.

I took a deep breath and surveyed my arm. "No," I said smartly. "It doesn't hurt."

"Good. That means it's working."

"What is all this about? Will one of y'all please tell me?"

"We really should have told her when she was younger," Rose said. "It wasn't right keeping this from her."

"Why in witch's name would anyone ever come to this godforsaken town?" Mama replied. "When Hildegarde the Swamp Witch said Charming would end up here, I knew the prophecy was wrong. The town was dying back then. No one would ever visit it—least of all a witch with puny magic."

"My magic isn't puny," I snapped. "No, I'm not as great as the Amazing Glinda." I gestured toward her. "Who *could* be with you and your traveling circus always trying to help people?"

Mama crossed her arms tightly. "Watch your mouth, Charming. I might be your mother, but I can still throw you over my knee. I know how to do that with my magic."

Anger twisted my gut to the point it hurt. "Would one of y'all explain what is going on?"

Rose hiked a shoulder. "You'd better do it, Glinda. The girl deserves to know."

"Yes, Mama," I said pointedly. "I deserve to know."

Mama sighed. She came around to my side of the car and leaned against the door. "When you were younger, we took you to the psychic. It's an old tradition, one steeped in ritual. It's important to know certain things about the child you've just borne. Or in some witch's cases, the baby you're carrying."

I shot her a questioning look.

She sighed. "Often a witch will go to the seer while the child is still *in utero*. Unfortunately I missed my first appointment and had to reschedule."

"Too busy saving the world?"

"I believe there was an undead outbreak in San Francisco that had to be dealt with." She sniffed. "Anyway, by the time I met with Hildegarde, you were already born. I gave her the boiled peanuts that helped her to see the baby's future, and that's when she told me."

"Told you what?"

She sighed. "Do we really have to discuss this now? We have a car full of panties and a Bigfoot to find."

I raised my glowing arm. "Yes, we have to discuss it now."

"Don't lose your temper."

I glared at her.

My mother expertly ignored my glare. "Hildegarde told me that you would be born with very little water witch power. That magic would be a part of your life but not all of it. As you can imagine, since you were born into a strong family of water witches, that was hard to hear."

I stared at my arm. "But I take it that wasn't all."

Mama shook her head. "No. It wasn't. Hildegarde told me that when the time came, you would enter the place of the forge—that's what she called it—and you would unite the powers of witchcraft."

"What?"

She sighed. "Really, Charming. When it comes to a prophecy, you have to read between the lines a bit. Uniting the powers means, I believe, that you'll be able to wield all four elements."

The glow faded, and my arm returned to normal. "Be able to wield all four elements? No one can do that."

Mama's shoulder ticked up. "It's extremely rare."

"The last known witch to be able to call on the four elements lived two hundred years ago, I believe," Rose said. "So it's possible. Just rare."

"But there's something wrong about it," I directed to Mama. "I know there is. You didn't want me to come here, and you sent Rose to watch over me."

Mama pinned her lips.

"What is it?" I pushed her. She was keeping information from me. I had to know what it was.

"All four elements are difficult to wield," she admitted. "You don't even appreciate magic, Charming. Why would I think you'd want that sort of power?"

I tapped my toe impatiently. "You're stalling. Tell me what's going on."

Mama shot Rose a look. Rose shrugged. "You might as well tell her."

My mother nodded. "Hildegarde revealed that if all your powers come in, it would be the beginning of the end for us witches."

I smirked. "Right. I get some powers and somehow that ends all witches? I don't buy it."

"It's true," my mother said. "Hildegarde is never wrong. For some

163

AMY BOYLES

reason, Charming—and I don't know why, but that's the prophecy—you obtaining the four elemental powers of witchcraft will put an end to magic as we know it."

I frowned. "But how can me getting my magic cause such a shift? It makes no sense."

Mama shook her head. "That's what we need to find out. I don't know much about prophecies, and I did my best to keep you away from this place. I never discussed it with you, and it wasn't like we ever came here for a family vacation."

At that moment every unkind word my mother had ever said hit me. "That's the reason you always put down my powers, isn't it? You wanted to keep me away from magic."

Mama sniffed. "Charming, I admit I've been horrible. I should have told you. Should have let you know the prophecy, but I was scared. So in my own way I did what I could to keep you from magic, as you said, because of the consequences. I thought if you were never interested in magic then you wouldn't pursue it. I was wrong."

I studied her, my chin trembling. "Are you sorry?"

She blinked. "Of course. It wasn't a good choice. Should I have you hate me or keep magic safe? I thought it would be best to have you hate me."

"You could've just told me." Anguish twisted my gut. For my entire life my mother had been just as torn up about our relationship as I had been, but I had never known the truth.

She wiped the back of her hand over her sniffling nose. "Can you ever find it in your heart to forgive me?"

I nodded. "Yes. I do. I love you."

"And I love you."

"Now," Mama said. Our gazes locked, and I felt a cold line fissure down my spine. "Charming, you have to stop accepting gifts from witches. The broom and pig were gifts. That has something to do with the elemental shift of power blossoming within you."

I grimaced. This whole thing was such a mess. "I'd hate to destroy magic, especially when I'm working so hard to help this place." My gaze swept back toward town and the vines of kudzu that threatened to strangle it. "Okay. I won't accept any more gifts."

"Good."

"But what about this magic? What about the power?"

"What about it?"

"Maybe it has a purpose," I suggested.

Mama gnawed the inside of her lip. She only did that whenever a situation perplexed her. "I worry that allowing you to learn your gifts will cause this shift to happen sooner rather than later."

But now I suddenly had real magic. Not just a little bit of match-making power. I had air and earth magic—at least that's what I figured. Broom had come from the air witches and Pig from Cap, who had earth magic. I hated to bring on doom and gloom, but I wanted to try out some of this power—learn how to wield it before all the magic in the world evaporated.

I shook my head. As if that was possible. Not that I didn't believe in prophecies, *but I didn't believe in prophecies*. At least not one so silly. All the magic in the world vanishing? I doubted that would happen.

But since my mother didn't appear interested in teaching me, I'd have to figure it out myself.

But first, a Bigfoot needed to be caught. Two Bigfoots, to be exact. After all, we didn't know if Emily's spell would turn deadly for Jimmy. In fact, I had a feeling it would.

The air shifted, and the scent of gardenia blossoms filled the night. The magic in this town was unstable, broken. The fact that Emily managed to create a working spell suggested that it would eventually sour, and when it did, my friend Jimmy would be on the receiving end of that.

I threw back my shoulders and raised my chin. "Come on, y'all. What are we standing around here for? We've got Bigfoot to catch."

TWENTY-THREE

We set up the panties on a line in the middle of the woods, not too far from the fire springs, where we'd seen Jimmy before.

"Mama, you'll have to be ready with your magic."

She nodded. "I will be. After all, I've vanquished greater enemies than this."

I rolled my eyes. "Of course you have. Just be ready."

My mother smiled, but I was worried. When Jimmy had run toward us before, she had frozen. Never in my life had I known my mother to freeze.

What was it about this place that was screwing with her brain? Was it the prophecy? Was it the fact that she was concerned her power wouldn't work correctly because of the laws of magic that affected so many people? Or was it something else?

Honestly, there was no time to worry about it because we needed to get into position.

"Let's go behind those bushes," Rose said.

It seemed as good as any other idea, so the five of us—don't forget Broom and Pig, though I made sure to stay far away from them— hunkered down behind the bushes.

After about two minutes Rose began to hum. "Ssshhh," I whispered. "You'll give us away."

"I'm bored," she whimpered. "Sitting here takes a lot of energy."

"Let's hope we won't have to do it long," Mama said.

A crash in the trees grabbed our attention. Our heads snapped toward it. I shot my mother and aunt a *be quiet* look and remained perfectly still.

A few seconds later Jimmy, covered from head to foot in fur, emerged from the forest. He took one look at the panties, threw his head back and howled.

Crap. The vampires would've definitely heard that.

"Now's our chance," Mama whispered. "Rose, help me restrain him with water bindings."

Rose nodded.

Jimmy paused, cocking his ear toward us. He took a step forward and sniffed. At least he was sniffing the air and not my clean underpants.

"Now," Mama yelled. She and Rose stood up and hit Jimmy with all the water magic they had. Water was pulled from the humid air. Long, thick ropes of it wound around his wrists.

"Hold him," Mama yelled.

Jimmy howled and snapped, but the binds held him tightly.

Something else crashed in the forest, and suddenly a second Bigfoot—this one must've been Emily—appeared.

My mother and aunt were too busy with Jimmy to stop it, so I had to take her on myself.

I held up my hand. I had no idea what I was doing. My magic was numbers and questions, it wasn't real elements.

I quickly calculated the odds that my new magic would falter and the Bigfoot would kill me. The odds that I would die were fifty to one.

Not very good.

But then suddenly a mound of earth shot up in front of the Bigfoot, stopping her from helping Jimmy. The creature whirled toward me and roared.

Mama yelled, "Charming!"

"Keep on Jimmy," I commanded. "I've got this one!"

The creature leaped over the mound of earth, and in that moment I realized something—I was screwed.

Like, literally.

The worst thing you can do when facing off against a predator is run, but I wasn't thinking clearly. The only thought that zipped through my head was that I needed to get the heck out of Dodge.

So I ran, crashing through the forest. The creature was taller, faster than I was, but something stirred in me. My feet kicked into high gear, and I was suddenly moving through the forest at high speed.

Air power. The gift of air magic made me fast—super fast, so fast I could outrun the creature.

Wait. Was it still behind me?

I paused long enough to hear twigs snap and branches ripping off trees.

Yep, she was still behind me.

The air was helping me, but I wouldn't be able to run forever. I could already feel the magic sputtering out.

I don't know why my mom thought some swamp woman's prophecy about me receiving my magic and then killing all magic in the world would come true when I couldn't even hold on to a little bit of running power.

Lights up ahead signaled I was almost back. The first hint of steel homes told me I was in Fire Town.

I broke free of the forest just as my newfound power petered out. I fell onto the ground and expected Emily to topple on me and maybe scratch me to death, but nothing happened.

In fact, the only thing that greeted me was silence.

I heaved myself off the ground, brushed off my pants and stared into the night. I waited, listening for a sound, any sound that would betray where the Bigfoot had gone.

Though I didn't hear any crunching, the sound of a door opening caught my attention.

Voices.

I followed the voices—one of which I recognized as Mayor Dixon.

"Emily, what are on earth are you doing out here? And without your clothes on?"

"Mayor." Emily sounded terrified. "The scariest thing just happened. I was attacked."

"What?" Mayor Dixon sounded frantic. "Who attacked you?"

I sneaked over to the side of the house and quietly tiptoed to the edge. I peered over the porch to see Emily, naked except for a blanket, bending over the mayor's outstretched arms.

"I'll tell you what happened when we get inside. But that match-maker, Mayor, she's the one causing all these problems."

My eyes flared. Are you kidding? Emily had shifted back to normal and was feeding lies to the mayor—lies that would get me thrown in jail.

"Come in, come in," the mayor said. Mayor Dixon glanced around as if to make sure some crazy person like myself wasn't about to jump out and attack her.

As if.

But I also didn't know what Emily's plan was. What if she was going inside the mayor's house in order to harm her? I couldn't let that happen. Absolutely not.

I had to think. I had to figure it out.

Surely Emily would know I'd figure out where she'd gone. Maybe she would count on it. If she counted on it, then she'd expect me to ring the doorbell and tell the mayor what I knew—which would put both of us head to head in a confrontation.

It would be her word against mine. I would lose.

Wouldn't I?

Unless the mayor had been suspecting something strange of Emily. If that was the case, then Emily might be in the house to attack the mayor.

For the goddess's sake, why didn't I just look to see what was going on?

I peered into a window. Emily sat on the couch. It looked like the mayor had gone into the kitchen, probably to get Emily something to calm her down.

I had to get inside without anyone knowing…but how?

"What are you doing out here snooping?"

I sucked air and whirled around, my head nearly spinning off I moved so fast.

Towering over me, a dark look on his face, stood Thorne. "Do I need to arrest you for being a peeping Tom?"

I glared at him. "No," I whispered. "It's Emily. She killed Langdon. She's another Bigfoot."

He cocked a curious brow. "Is she, now?"

"Yes. She chased me. My mother and aunt have Jimmy in the forest." I watched him, but Thorne didn't reveal an expression of surprise. My voice faltered. "You already know this, don't you?"

He nodded. "My men have him. Your mother sent me this way. Your aunt and mother are helping my men."

"Vampires need help from witches?"

I think he growled. I stared at him. "Emily's inside. I'm afraid she's going to hurt the mayor if we barge in."

His gaze flickered to the window. "I need to slip inside."

"*We* do," I corrected.

He opened his mouth to argue but then shut it. I guess Thorne had already figured out he couldn't argue with me and win.

"There's a rose trellis on the other side of the house," he said.

"I'm right behind you."

Thorne climbed the trellis like a native and in one swift movement, he had the window open and had slipped through.

Me, on the other hand, I found the trellis harder to climb than expected. I did my best not to pant and heave, but I still did, and in the end Thorne hoisted me through the opening like I was nothing more than a pillow.

Warning flashed in his eyes. "Stay back. Be quiet."

We slipped soundlessly from the upstairs bedroom to the hallway.

"It was that matchmaker," Emily was saying. "You have to fire her and tell Thorne what she's done."

"I will," Mayor Dixon said calmly. "Just tell me everything."

As Emily started to talk, I watched Thorne. He looked as concerned as I was. It was the same dilemma; would the mayor's life be in danger if we showed up?

"Let me see if I can call Thorne," Winnifred said. "My phone's in the kitchen."

Thorne pointed two fingers at me and then to the floor, which I assumed meant stay where I was.

I would. Sort of.

Thorne disappeared down the stairwell. The mayor shrieked, it sounded like wood splintered and then Emily's voice, much deeper, filled the house.

"Make one move, vampire, and I'll kill her," Emily said.

Oh great, Thorne's plan hadn't gone the way he wanted. I stepped slowly down the stairs and peered into the living room.

Emily's back was to me. She stood tall, in Bigfoot form. She had one hand on the mayor's neck. Thorne stared her down, his fingers flexing as if he wanted to wring her throat.

"And I thought I'd just be dealing with a meddlesome matchmaker," she said. "But it looks like now things have gotten complicated."

"But why, Emily?" the mayor croaked. "Why are you doing this?"

"Isn't it obvious? I told you my family had been cursed but I didn't say how. I'm a Bigfoot. It's my curse. But I'm blessed in that my magic lets me make other Bigfoots. And I need a mate."

She kept talking. "At first I thought Langdon would make a good mate, so I turned him into a Bigfoot but he was stupid. Then Langdon threatened to tell others what I had done—he was unstable, so I killed him."

I cringed. Emily really had some issues.

But me thinking about Emily wasn't going to stop the madness in front of me. If Thorne moved, Emily would crush the mayor's throat.

He might be a vampire, and a killer at that, but I didn't think Thorne wanted the mayor to die.

I could help. I had some power, even though it was waning. But I didn't really know how to wield it, so what good was I? I glanced to my right. There sat a heavy silver candelabra. If I could pick it up and smash it over Emily's head, that would help.

Of course, Emily was also eight feet tall now. Not exactly a featherweight opponent.

Right as I was trying to figure out a way to help the mayor, a squealing pig ran from the kitchen into the living room.

"What in the...?" Emily said, distracted.

Pig ran between her legs. Emily whirled around. I picked up the candelabra and smashed it against her face.

Emily dropped the mayor, and quick as lightning, Thorne had the howling Bigfoot wrestled to the ground.

A second later, half a dozen law enforcement officers crashed into the house, helping Thorne handcuff Emily and make sure the mayor was okay.

~

A LITTLE WHILE later I stood outside, the warm summer air sending the smell of flowering gardenias up my nose.

Mayor Winnifred Dixon shot me a weary smile. I crossed to her and wrapped an arm over her shoulder. "If you'd wanted me to matchmake Bigfoot, why didn't you just say so?"

She laughed.

Pig ran up to me, snorting happily. I scooped her into my arms and gave the swine a squeeze. "You did good, Pig."

Mama rushed in with Rose following behind her. "Charming, are you okay?"

I nodded. "I'm fine, and thank y'all. If you hadn't sent Pig in to rescue us, I'm not sure what would've happened."

"What are mothers for?" Mama ran her hands over me to make sure I was telling the truth and wasn't really hurt. "But in the forest, how'd you get away from the creature?"

A whimsical smile danced on my lips. "Why, magic of course."

Mama's eyebrow practically coiled around her nose it arched so dramatically. "You used the magic?"

"Yep, I used the magic. Granted, I didn't exactly know what I was doing, but it worked out okay."

"Charming…"

"Don't worry," I said soothingly. "I know you're worried about the prophecy. I won't do anything to mess up magic for the rest of the world."

She glared at me.

"I promise."

"Pig," Aunt Rose declared. "You saved the day."

I handed Pig to Rose, who pulled a chocolate bar from her pocket and gave it to the snorting animal. "Yep. Looks like she's a great addition to our little gang."

Broom swiveled around impatiently. I laughed. "You too, Broom. No one's forgetting about you."

Broom dipped into a bow.

"Miss Calhoun!"

My breath caught in my throat at the sight of Jimmy running toward me. He wasn't a Bigfoot anymore, he was human, and someone had been kind enough to find clothes for him. They were a bit big, the shirt hanging off his shoulders and the pants rolled up to the ankles, but Jimmy was safe.

I rushed over and threw my arms around his neck. "Jimmy! You're okay."

"Thanks to you, Miss Calhoun."

My hands slid down his arms as we parted. I gripped his hands and smiled so wide my face nearly cracked in two. "Jimmy, I'm so sorry all of this happened."

He raked his fingers through his wavy brown hair. "None of this is your fault. I'm sorry I let you down."

I stared at him, shocked he would say such a thing. "You didn't let me down. I let you down by sending you to a town where you were turned into Bigfoot and placed under a spell that could've killed you."

He shook his head. "It's not your fault. I went sticking my nose in places and then got spelled by Emily. I'm just glad y'all caught her."

I cocked my head at an angle that suggested I was confused, which

I was. "But how'd you change back?"

"Emily changed me. She didn't want to, but your mom shoved a mandrake root in her hand and told her to do it."

I glanced at my mother and shot her a look of appreciation that she didn't see. My mother, for all her quirks and pompous attitude, had saved the day.

"Jimmy, first thing in the morning, why don't you go home? I'll work on this project here."

Excitement radiated across his face. "You mean it, Miss Calhoun?"

"I sure do."

I gave Jimmy another hug before he walked back to the medical truck.

A dark shadow stretched across the pavement beside me. I didn't have to look up to know who it was.

"You did well tonight," Thorne admitted.

I cocked my chin at him in arrogance. "Was that so hard?"

Mischief danced in his silvery eyes. "Was what so hard?"

"Admitting I helped and that I can be of service?"

"Yes."

We stared at each other before we each cracked a smile. Thorne chuckled and I swear it was one of the most pleasant sounds I'd ever heard.

What was wrong with me? Vampires weren't pleasant.

"Thank you for your help. So, I guess you'll be leaving town soon?"

"Does the thought excite you?" I said.

His voice deepened. Our gazes locked, and a sliver of energy zipped straight to my stomach. "You have no idea what excites me."

For some reason I had the idea he was suggesting something to do with me. The air thickened with tension. I cleared my throat and looked away.

"No, I won't be leaving." I took a step forward and leaned so close my lips nearly grazed his throat. I whispered, "And you have no idea what excites me, either."

I retreated a step, threw him a wink and walked back to my family, who were ready to go home.

TWENTY-FOUR

The police released Cap the next day. I had my next move all planned out and had convinced Belinda to quench the mandrake spell.

"I don't understand why I need to be here, Charming," the mayor huffed.

I tapped a pen on my matchmaking folder. "Just you wait. There's something I want you to witness."

Belinda stood by the tavern doors. She worried her lips nervously.

"It's going to be okay," I whispered. "Just hold on."

"What is?" Mayor Winnifred Dixon asked.

"All of it. This town, if I'm right."

She blotted a handkerchief over her throat. "Right about what?"

The doors opened, and Cap strode out. "This," I said.

He took one look at Belinda, and his face filled with longing and want. My heart lurched for them. At the same moment my heart leaped to my gizzard, Cap took two long strides toward Belinda, wove his fingers through her dark hair, dipped her down and gave her the kiss to end all kisses.

"What is that?" the mayor said.

A light haloed Belinda and Cap. The ground rumbled, and it was like the energy emanating from them was washing the town clean. The grime faded, the kudzu receded and Witch's Forge opened to the public once more.

I pointed at Cap and Belinda. "That is the solution to your problems. I don't know if Witch's Forge is back to normal, but I have a feeling the falls have opened and now you can get regular folks in here again. But first"—I pointed a finger at her—"you've got to dispel that horrible law that witches and wizards of different magics can't marry. They need to marry. The blight on this town was caused by too much magical inbreeding."

The mayor's jaw dropped. She raised her hand, and a sheet of paper appeared in front of her.

She jumped back, screaming, "Ah!"

I smirked. "Not used to your magic doing what you ask, are you?"

"No, I'm not." She stared at the piece of paper. "This is the law that our founding fathers created."

I clapped a hand on her shoulder. "With all due respect, the founding fathers were wrong. Witches need to marry wizards of different magic. It's important."

Mayor Dixon stared at the paper before taking it in her fingers and ripping it apart.

"From now on," the mayor proclaimed, "everyone can marry whoever they want." She quickly turned to me, fear in her eyes. "But you're not finished here yet, are you, Charming? You're still under contract."

I smiled. "Don't you worry, Mayor. When I arrived, I thought this was the worst hillbilly town I'd ever stepped foot in." My gaze landed on Thorne, who studied me before turning away. "But now I think it's A-okay."

"Well done, Charming. Now if you'll excuse me, I have a town to ready." The mayor walked off, clapping. "Attention, everyone, Witch's Forge is now open for business. Tourists—humans are coming. We must be ready."

I crossed my arms and smiled, delighted in my handiwork.

"Charming." My mother popped up beside me. "Looks like you've done well."

I squeezed her arm. "Great. Now you can leave and return to your life. I'm sure there's a Nepalese village in need of your training."

She shook her head. "Oh no. I'm staying. Remember, the prophecy."

I clicked my tongue. "Right."

"I won't leave until you do."

Great.

Rose walked up with Pig on a leash. "Charming, what you've done here is great. Now if y'all don't mind, Pig and I are hungry. I've got a meal back at the house. Anyone care to join me?"

I wrapped my arm over her shoulder. "I'd love to."

We started to walk away when someone calling my name, *again*, caught my attention.

"Charming!"

Kimberly ran up to me. She clasped my hands. "Charming, the train is arriving. I just got an alert."

I quirked a brow. "An alert?"

Her cheeks crimsoned. "I have one of my cousins on lookout. Do you think my soul mate is on it?"

I glanced at my file folder. "I'm not sure. Maybe we should check it out."

Kimberly clapped. "I'm so excited. Let's go meet my soul mate!"

I straightened and threw my head back. "Lead the way, Kimberly. Take me to the train station."

ALSO BY AMY BOYLES

SWEET TEA WITCH MYSTERIES
SOUTHERN MAGIC
SOUTHERN SPELLS
SOUTHERN MYTHS
SOUTHERN SORCERY
SOUTHERN CURSES
SOUTHERN KARMA
SOUTHERN MAGIC THANKSGIVING
SOUTHERN MAGIC CHRISTMAS
SOUTHERN POTIONS
SOUTHERN FORTUNES
SOUTHERN HAUNTINGS
SOUTHERN WANDS

SOUTHERN GHOST WRANGLER MYSTERIES
SOUL FOOD SPIRITS
HONEYSUCKLE HAUNTING
THE GHOST WHO ATE GRITS
BACKWOODS BANSHEE

BLESS YOUR WITCH SERIES
SCARED WITCHLESS
KISS MY WITCH
QUEEN WITCH
QUIT YOUR WITCHIN'
FOR WITCH'S SAKE

DON'T GIVE A WITCH

WITCH MY GRITS

FRIED GREEN WITCH

SOUTHERN WITCHING

Y'ALL WITCHES

HOLD YOUR WITCHES

SOUTHERN SINGLE MOM PARANORMAL MYSTERIES

The Witch's Handbook to Hunting Vampires

The Witch's Handbook to Catching Werewolves

The Witch's Handbook to Trapping Demons

ABOUT THE AUTHOR

Hey, I'm Amy,

I write books for folks who crave laugh-out-loud paranormal mysteries. I help bring humor into readers' lives. I've got a Pharm D in pharmacy, a BA in Creative Writing and a Masters in Life.

And when I'm not writing or chasing around two small children (one of which is four going on thirteen), I can be found antique shopping for a great deal, getting my roots touched up (because that's an every four week job) and figuring out when I can get back to Disney World.

If you're dying to know more about my wacky life, here are three things you don't know about me.

—In college I spent a semester at Marvel Comics working in the X-Men office.

—I worked at Carnegie Hall.

—I grew up in a barbecue restaurant—literally. My parents owned one.

If you want to reach out to me—and I love to hear from readers— you can email me at amyboylesauthor@gmail.com.

Happy reading!